The Marked:
Crimson Rising

Olivia Paisley Troy

1

When skin is branded, truth is chained,
When silence blooms where hope is slain,
One crimson spark will split the sky—
A mark to rise, or mark to die.

Prologue

They tell us the Marks are truth.
That a single streak of color across the wrist is more
certain than blood, more binding than bone.

Green for longevity.
Amber for note.
Blue for service.
Crimson for violence.

The Dominion says it is mercy—knowing the shape
of your death before it comes. They call it order,
destiny, a gift wrapped in firelight and steel. They say
it keeps chaos from the streets and rebellion from the
shadows.

But those who bear the Crimson know better.
We are not warnings.
We are weapons.

I was thirteen when the scanner burned my skin red.
The crowd hushed, as if the air itself was holding its
breath. The official stamped my name into the
registry, already less a girl than a countdown.

Four birthday have passed since then.
I am seventeen now.
And the Dominion is still watching.

What they don't know is that I am watching too.

Chapter 1

Marked and Counted

The first thing I feel when I wake is the throbbing in my wrist.

It's faint, like the pulse of something buried too deep to reach, yet insistent enough to drag me out of uneasy sleep. My Crimson Mark. The Dominion calls it a designation, a "predictive identifier" stamped into me at thirteen. I call it a countdown.

Today, the countdown ticks louder.

Because today is **Recount Day**.

The entire city will line up, citizen by citizen, to be scanned and measured, their biometric patterns compared against last year's data. The Dominion likes its records precise. They like to remind us that nothing slips past their eyes—not our health, not our behavior, not our fate.

I rub the skin just above the Mark, as though I can muffle its glow through sheer stubbornness. The small square scarlet emblem is etched into the underside of my wrist, impossible to cover with anything less than a full sleeve. It isn't raised, but it radiates a strange warmth whenever my pulse races. A warning system, almost, reminding me what color I belong to.

Crimson. Violent death before the age of nineteen.

Seventeen now. My birthday just passed last month, quiet and uncelebrated, because the fewer people who know you're a Crimson, the better.

"Up, Elia." My aunt's voice drifts through the thin walls of our narrow flat. Calm, firm, with the faint rasp that comes from spending nights grinding roots and drying herbs over smoke. "The Recount queue will stretch the entire city if you linger."

I groan and push myself upright. The mattress sighs beneath me, its springs older than I am. Our home is wedged in one of New Virelia's residential stacks— rows of concrete towers identical in shape, numbering only in their surveillance beacons. Outside my narrow window, the gray sky hums with the sound of patrol drones slicing through morning fog. Their wings pulse blue as they scan rooftops for unregistered movement.

Every Recount Day begins like this: a city taut with nerves, people brushing dust off their neatest clothes, the silent rhythm of fear.

I tug on my shirt—a plain charcoal tunic that covers my wrists. A patched jacket follows, sleeves tugged low. The Dominion says we should display our Marks openly, that acceptance is strength. But even the boldest Greens and Blues keep theirs tucked away. For Crimsons, concealment is survival.

I splash cold water on my face in the cracked basin. The reflection that stares back at me is sharper than I feel: angular jaw, dark eyes that look too serious for someone who hasn't even finished school. My hair—thick, black, and stubbornly wavy—falls against my cheekbones. I consider braiding it back but leave it loose; braids draw attention, and today I need to be invisible.

When I step into the kitchen, my aunt already has the kettle steaming. The air smells faintly of valerian and sage. She keeps jars of herbs on a shelf disguised as "kitchen seasonings," though her real work is far from culinary.

"You slept poorly again." She doesn't phrase it as a question.

"The Mark kept me awake."

Her eyes soften, though the lines around her mouth deepen. "Then you'll need calm for today. Drink."

She pours a thin stream of golden tea into a clay cup and slides it across the table. Chamomile, with something sharper beneath—one of her blends that soothes nerves and slows a racing heartbeat. Dominion medscans can't detect herbs in your system, not if prepared properly. That's my aunt's talent: quiet defiance in the form of remedies that slip through surveillance cracks.

I sip obediently, though the taste is bitter. "It won't change the scan."

"No," she admits. "But it may change you."

Her gaze lingers on me, steady, protective, and shadowed with grief that never really left. She's been my guardian since the day my parents vanished. No explanations. No official records. Just gone. I was thirteen, fresh from my first Marking Ceremony, my wrist still raw from the Dominion's branded implant. They told me Crimson, and days later my parents disappeared into the night.

Some children believed their parents abandoned them out of shame. I never believed that. Not once.

I just learned not to ask why too loudly.

The streets are alive by the time we step out, a restless current pulling everyone toward the square. My aunt keeps her steady pace beside me. Families cluster tight, shoulders brushing as if the closeness might protect them. Most people keep their heads bowed, though every so often someone can't help glancing upward—toward the drones, toward the watchful sky.

Above us, a cluster of Dominion drones hums in perfect formation, their frames a polished silver like insects born of steel. Blue light scans every moving figure, registering implants, confirming identification codes.

Billboards flicker on the side of towers as we pass:

THE DOMINION SEES.
THE DOMINION PROTECTS.
OBEDIENCE IS STRENGTH.

I keep my head angled downward, gaze fixed on the cracks in the pavement. Eye contact with a surveillance lens can trigger an evaluation. So can fidgeting. So can lingering too long in a shadow.

Most of all, a Crimson can't appear *dangerous*. Dominion algorithms measure aggression by muscle tension, micro-expressions, even the way you breathe. Harmlessness must be performed with precision.

We join the line curling through the city square. People file toward the biometric scanners, sleek black gates erected overnight by Dominion operatives. Each gate glows faintly, a vertical bar of light from floor to arch. Citizens step forward, extend their wrists, and wait for the pulse of recognition: green for cleared, amber for note, blue is meant to serve, and red for warning.

The queue moves in heavy silence broken only by drone hums. I tug my sleeves lower, willing my heartbeat to slow.

"Do you remember your first scan?" my aunt murmurs beside me.

The words drag me backward in time.

I was thirteen, still trembling from the Marking Ceremony where the Dominion seared the Crimson onto my wrist. They lined us up afterward for our first Recount. Rows of children, eyes wide, wrists still raw, waiting for the machine to declare us properly cataloged.

When my turn came, the scanner lit crimson, an ugly flare across the square. The crowd inhaled sharply.

That night, my parents whispered fiercely to each other while I pretended to sleep. My mother's voice broke. My father's hands shook. Three days later, they were gone.

And I never stopped wondering if the two were linked.

"Yes," I whisper to my aunt. "I remember."

She squeezes my hand once. "Then remember also: you survived it."

We near the front of the line. My stomach knots. Each scan takes only seconds: a wrist pressed against the console, a flicker of light, the machine confirming that Dominion's predictions still align with your biology.

A boy my age goes before me. His Mark is amber. His scan glows yellow, and the agent waves him aside for "monitoring." His mother squeezes his shoulder as if to hide her fear.

Then it's my turn.

I step forward, my heartbeat so loud it drowns out the drone hums. The Dominion agent doesn't even glance at me at first—just the computer in front of him, uniform so black it seems to swallow the light. The silver emblem on his chest gleams like a warning.

"Wrist," he says, clipped, practiced.

I tug back my sleeve. The Crimson square pulses faintly, as if it knows what's coming.

The scanner hums to life. A red flare cuts across the console.

Only then does the agent look up. His eyes are empty, glassy, the kind of stare you get from years of training yourself not to care. "Biometric patterns show irregularities."

My throat goes dry.

He types something into his computer; lips pressed into a thin line. "Proceed." His tone carries no warmth.

But I know what it means to be flagged.

I step out of the scanner, my body trembling with the effort to appear calm. My aunt's hand brushes my back, steady but firm. She doesn't speak until we're clear of the square.

"Keep your pace normal," she whispers as we weave through the dispersing crowd. "Drones read patterns. No sudden movements."

I obey. My chest feels like it's caving in, but my strides remain even, careful. The hum overhead confirms it: drones have begun trailing us. Not directly—never directly—but close enough that I feel their presence like a shadow.

Something shifted today—I can feel it, even if I can't name what.

The Dominion doesn't flag people on a whim. They never have.

And once their eyes are on you, they don't look away. Not until there's nothing left to uncover.

Chapter 2

The Unseen and the Watched

New Virelia always looks cleaner after Recount Day.

The Dominion likes things spotless, and squads of utility drones sweep through every city before dawn, scrubbing walls, hosing down pavement, purging graffiti or chalk-drawn games that children dared to scrawl in back alleys. By the time morning light filters through the gray haze, the city looks almost antiseptic—like a sterile stage where every actor must play their role.

But no matter how polished the streets, you can taste the tension in the air afterward. People walk tighter, shoulders hunched, as if afraid the scanners followed them home. Markets are quieter, and laughter—what little there ever is in public—seems forced, brittle, like glass ready to shatter.

And today, the air feels even heavier. Because I was flagged.

I pull my jacket tighter, the sleeves dragging past my wrists. The Crimson Mark beneath thrums faintly, like it knows I've drawn unwanted notice. I can almost feel the drones watching, though none hover close enough to make it obvious. That's the Dominion's favorite trick: you never know if they're staring at you until it's too late.

The market square sits at the center of our residential city, a rectangle of cracked stone surrounded by steel-frame stalls. Vendors set up early, but goods are limited. The Dominion regulates supplies down to the ounce, and "luxuries" like fruit or bread vanish within hours. My aunt trades herbs here, quiet and discreet, her jars labeled with kitchen-friendly names that won't draw suspicion: thyme, basil, rosemary. Only those who know her reputation ask for the hidden remedies—teas for sleep, poultices for fevers, tinctures to ease the body when Dominion meds fail or cost too much.

I come here every few days, running errands, but never lingering. Eyes are everywhere. The Dominion encourages citizens to report "unusual behavior," and the threat works; neighbors whisper about each other behind shutters, and paranoia blooms like weeds between the cracks of every conversation.

Today, the paranoia feels sharper. A hush clings to the air, and conversations end abruptly whenever drones pass overhead. A woman selling root vegetables lowers her voice when I approach, muttering about "attacks on the northern perimeter." She doesn't elaborate. No one dares.

The word hangs there anyway: **rebels**.

It's spoken only in fragments, like a superstition— half-acknowledged, half-denied. They say rebels strike outposts on the outskirts, that they smuggle contraband into the city, that they burn Dominion records. Some whisper they're former Dominion officers gone rogue, others claim they're unmarked children who fled before their ceremonies, living free in the wilds beyond the perimeter.

But no one speaks too loudly. Because to admit the rebels exist is to admit the Dominion doesn't control everything.

And the Dominion cannot allow that.

I pick up a bundle of stale bread, weighing it against the ration tokens in my pouch. When I hand the tokens over, the vendor's hand brushes mine deliberately. A sliver of something slips between my fingers, so small I almost miss it.

I glance up. The boy behind the stall is maybe my age, with hair falling into his eyes and an expression too casual, like he's trying hard not to look at me. His lips twitch in what might be the ghost of a smile.

Before I can react, a drone hums past overhead. My heart jerks, and I shove my hand into my jacket pocket.

The sliver warms against my skin, then breaks apart, gray ash sifting through my fingers. For a heartbeat I think it's gone—just dust. But then letters flicker across my palm, glowing as though branded straight into flesh:

THE MARK DOESN'T DEFINE YOU. WE SEE YOU.

My breath catches. Too fast, too loud. And then, just as quickly, the words dissolve, leaving only a faint itch, like heat after a burn.

I whip my gaze back to the vendor, but he's busy stacking bread, expression blank, as if nothing unusual happened.

A shiver runs through me.

That was no ordinary flyer. It was coded—rebellion tech, the kind whispered about but never seen. Messages that erase themselves, designed to slip through Dominion surveillance nets.

And somehow, one just landed in my hand.

I force my expression flat, calm. The Dominion watches everything: posture, breath, even the dilation of pupils. They'll notice curiosity like blood in the water.

I keep my eyes low, trade a few more tokens for potatoes, and move along. The ash has already blown away, leaving no evidence. Still, my heart pounds against my ribs like it wants to escape.

Rebels know who I am.

Or at least... they saw my wrist. Crimson.

We see you.

The words echo like a promise. Or a threat.

I head back toward our flat, gripping the basket tighter than necessary. I keep rehearsing excuses in my head: *If my aunt notices, I'll say nothing. If drones scan, I'll look harmless. If anyone asks, I'll pretend I never saw a thing.*

That's the only way to survive here: suppress every spark of curiosity.

Because curiosity gets punished.

I've seen it before. A neighbor two floors down asked too many questions about the Dominion's food shipments—where they came from, why the portions shrank every month. Three days later, his door was sealed shut, and his family was relocated. No explanation. Just gone.

The Dominion doesn't need explanations. Fear is explanation enough.

I'm halfway home when the public screens light up.

Every city has them—massive silver panels affixed to towers, visible from every street corner. They flicker on without warning, broadcasting the Dominion's message across the city.

A familiar face fills the screen: Commander Hyran, head of New Virelia's internal security. His voice is smooth, polished, unnervingly calm.

"Citizens of New Virelia," he begins, eyes glinting like steel. "In light of recent unrest at our northern perimeter, the Dominion reminds you of your duty. Report all suspicious behavior immediately, especially from those whose Marks place them at risk of instability. Crimsons, in particular, are known to act unpredictably under stress. Protect your community. Protect the Dominion. Report what you see."

My stomach clenches. Around me, the crowd stiffens, glances cutting sideways. It's subtle, but I know what they're thinking: *Which of us is Crimson? Which of us is unstable?*

The broadcast ends as abruptly as it began. The screen goes black.

And the silence afterward is deafening.

I walk faster, pulse racing.

The Dominion never airs messages by accident. If they're warning against rebels, it means rebel activity is closer than anyone thought. And if they're warning against Crimsons—against me—then maybe that boy's message wasn't coincidence. Maybe I've already been noticed.

By the time I reach the narrow alleys near our block, my palms are slick with sweat.

And that's when I see him.

Not clearly. Just a figure leaning in the shadow of a crumbling wall, where the alley forks near the water pipes. At first I think he's just another loiterer, until I notice the ink.

A raven tattoo sprawls across the side of his neck, black wings etched with sharp precision. It glints faintly in the dim light.

And for a moment—just a flicker—my implant glitches.

Everyone in New Virelia has an ID signal, coded into our implants. Drones pick it up instantly, displaying name, age, and Mark color. But as I glance at him, my vision stutters, static flooding the edges. No ID registers. No color.

Like the Dominion can't see him.

I blink hard, and the glitch vanishes. My implant resets, displaying the names of two passing workers, their Marks flashing green. But the raven-marked figure is gone, like smoke fading into air.

I stand frozen, breath caught, until a drone hum makes me flinch. Then I hurry home, heart thudding like I've swallowed a drum.

That night, I lie awake in the narrow bed. The city outside hums with distant patrols, blue light flashing across my curtains every time a drone sweeps past.

I tell myself I imagined it. That the boy at the market was reckless, that the flyer was just ash, that the man with the raven tattoo never stood in the alley.

But deep down, I know I didn't dream it.

Hours later, after drifting into that thin, restless sleep, a sound yanks me awake—the faintest creak.

My door. Opening.

I freeze under the blanket, lungs aching from holding my breath. Shadows shift in the kitchen, moving slow, deliberate. A drawer slides. A cabinet clicks shut.

Then silence. Nothing stolen. Nothing broken.

By dawn the flat looks the same, and my aunt hums over her tea as if the night never happened.

But I know better.

Someone was here.

Not searching for herbs.

Searching for me.

Chapter 3

Whispers in the Smoke

The morning after the search, the air in New Virelia feels sharper, like every breath cuts at the throat.

Nothing in our flat looks disturbed. My aunt moves about as usual, grinding herbs, boiling water for tea. But I know what I heard. The faint scrape of boots on the kitchen floor. The quiet slide of drawers. Someone was here, and whoever it was left no trace.

The Dominion is precise like that. They don't need to take anything to remind you they can enter your home whenever they please.

Still, I keep silent. My aunt has enough to worry about without me adding paranoia to her already guarded life. Instead, I sip the bitter tea she hands me and force myself to swallow calm.

But the Mark on my wrist won't let me forget. It pulses faintly, as if reminding me: **you are not safe.**

By the time I reach the city market that afternoon, whispers coil through the air like smoke. People gather in clumps, speaking in voices hushed but urgent. Vendors keep glancing at the corners of the square, where drones hover closer than usual, their blue beams flickering.

I don't mean to listen, but fragments catch on the wind.

"…another one gone…"
"…his family says he never came back from the Recount…"
"…Crimson, wasn't he?"

The word claws at me. Crimson.

I edge closer to a group of older women haggling over root vegetables. They speak low, heads bent, but their words slice through the hum of the square.

"Dax Halvern," one whispers. "Seventeen. Crimson since thirteen."

My chest tightens. Dax.

I know that name.

Once, years ago, Dax lived only three blocks from me. We were children together, climbing the rusted ladders of the water towers, daring each other to run past the drone beacons before curfew. He was lanky, loud, always laughing. The kind of boy who made you forget the Dominion even existed—until the day of our Marking.

I got Crimson. So did he. We didn't laugh after that.

I haven't seen him in months. And now… gone?

"Vanished after his last Recount," another woman says, voice trembling. "The Dominion claims relocation. But we all know what that means."

They fall silent as a drone passes overhead, its camera whirring. Then the women scatter, pretending to shop.

I stand frozen, the name burning in my ears.

Dax. Vanished into silence, the same kind that swallowed my parents.

That night, I can't hold the words inside. I tell my aunt, voice low, as she presses dried valerian into small packets for barter.

"They say Dax Halvern's gone. He was Crimson, like me."

Her hands still, the thin paper crinkling. Slowly, she looks up, her eyes shadowed.

"Elia," she says softly, "you must stop listening to whispers."

"But—"

"No." She cuts me off with a shake of her head. "Crimson means danger. To them, and to you. Don't ask questions you cannot afford the answers to."

Her voice is firm, but beneath it I hear the same fear I've carried for years. The fear that I'll vanish too.

I stare at the packets lined neatly on the table, my throat tight. "So we just… keep our heads down? Pretend it doesn't happen?"

"That is how we survive," she says.

But survival feels thinner every day.

Later, when I lie awake in my narrow bed, the question gnaws at me: are these disappearances accidents—or purges?

The Dominion calls it relocation, but everyone knows that's a lie. People marked Crimson don't come back. They slip out of sight, quietly, too cleanly—like the city erases them with one sweep. Dax. My parents. How many others are already gone, their names fading before anyone dares speak them?

And still, we pretend not to see.

That night, sleep drags me into fog.

I'm small again—thirteen, standing in the afterglow of the Marking Ceremony. The air smells like metal and smoke. My wrist burns, raw with the fresh Crimson.

Through the haze, I see my mother. She's crying, her hand clamped over her mouth. My father's arm is around her shoulders, but he looks broken, like someone carved the strength out of him.

Then another voice, deep and harsh, slices through the dream:

"She wasn't meant to be Crimson." The voice slices through the dream, too sharp to ignore.

I jolt awake, breath ragged. My sheets cling damp to my skin.

The words echo, too sharp to be imagination. I don't remember anyone saying them that day. But maybe I was too dazed, too young to understand.

She wasn't supposed to be Crimson.

What did that mean?

The next day, I return to the square to trade herbs. The air stinks of charred wood.

One of the stalls has been burned out, its frame blackened, smoke still curling from the ashes. People skirt around it nervously, whispering.

I pause, staring at the ruin. Someone torched it deliberately—the Dominion's drones would never allow fire by accident.

And then I see it.

Amid the scorched boards, a fragment of cloth clings to the frame. Letters etched in soot, faint but unmistakable:

CRIMSON IS A KEY, NOT A CURSE.

My breath catches.

Another rebel message. Left in plain sight this time, daring the Dominion to erase it.

I glance around quickly. No one else seems to notice—or if they do, they pretend not to. The drones hover close, their blue beams bright. Within minutes, the stall will be dismantled, the words scrubbed.

But I saw them.

And the meaning sparks through me like fire.

Maybe it isn't a curse at all. Maybe it's a key.

The Dominion has always told me Crimson means death. But what if it means something more?

Work runs late. My aunt has me deliver a bundle of herbs to a client near the southern stacks. By the time I finish, dusk drapes over the city, the sky bruised purple.

The streets are nearly empty. Curfew approaches.

That's when I hear the footsteps.

At first, I think I'm imagining it—the echo of my own boots on the cracked pavement. But then the rhythm splits. Two sets. Heavier. Following.

I glance back.

Two Dominion enforcers, black uniforms gleaming faintly in the streetlight. Their faces are hidden behind mirrored visors, but their pace matches mine perfectly.

Panic spikes in my chest.

I quicken my stride. They quicken too.

My pulse hammers. I duck into an alley, weaving between rusted pipes and crumbling walls. Shadows stretch long in the dim light. The enforcers follow, their boots striking hard.

"Citizen!" one calls, voice distorted by the visor. "Halt for inspection!"

I run.

The alley twists, narrow and jagged. My breath rasps, but adrenaline drives me forward. I vault a broken crate, skid around a corner. Behind me, metal clatters—one of them tripped, but the other is still close.

Blue light flickers on the walls as a drone swoops low, scanning. I duck beneath its beam, heart seizing, and plunge deeper into the maze of alleys.

For a moment, I think I'm trapped—the path dead-ends at a rusted fence. My chest tightens. But then I spot a gap near the bottom, just wide enough.

I drop to the ground, scraping my hands raw as I wriggle through. The enforcer's shout echoes behind me, but by the time he reaches the fence, I'm gone, sprinting through another passage.

I don't stop until I reach the back door of our flat, lungs burning.

I slam the door shut, chest heaving. My aunt rushes from the kitchen, alarm flashing across her face.

"Elia—?"

But before I can answer, my wrist ignites.

The Crimson Mark glows bright, red light pulsing beneath the skin. My implant buzzes sharply, static flooding my vision for a split second.

And then a voice, low and mechanical, rasps from a hidden speaker somewhere in the walls:

"You're being watched, Elia Dareth."

The glow fades. Silence drops heavy.

I stare at my wrist, trembling.

Whoever it was—Dominion, rebels, or something else—they know my name.

And they are already inside my life.

Chapter 4

The Stranger with the Raven Tattoo

Routine checks are never routine.

That's the first lesson you learn in New Virelia.

They happen at random, Dominion agents sweeping a block or pulling citizens aside at the market, always with the same calm precision. "Routine check," they say, as if it's as harmless as counting inventory. But everyone knows better.

Because sometimes people don't come back.

It happens just as I'm leaving the southern square, my basket half-filled with the day's meager rations. Dusk is settling in, curfew not far off. I keep my eyes down, movements careful, trying to look like any other citizen.

Then the shadow falls across my path.

Two Dominion agents step out from the corner, blocking the alley. Their uniforms are obsidian black, polished helmets reflecting the dim light. Each carries the standard-issue pulse baton at their side, though it's the injector strapped to their belts that makes my stomach seize.

"Citizen," one says, voice muffled by his visor. "Routine check."

My mouth goes dry. "I—I've already been scanned this week."

The agent's head tilts, like a machine parsing data. "Step forward."

I hesitate only a fraction, then obey. To resist would be worse. I place my basket down slowly, keeping my hands visible.

The second agent reaches for my wrist. His grip is firm, gloved fingers tightening as he yanks my sleeve upward.

The Crimson Mark flares under the streetlight.

A hush falls over the alley, heavy and dangerous.

"Crimson," the first agent mutters. "Flagged subject."

The second is already reaching for his injector. The needle glints faintly, filled with something clear. My pulse spikes—what do they inject? Sedatives? Trackers? I don't want to find out.

"Hold her," he orders.

Panic claws up my throat. I jerk back, struggling, but the agent's grip is iron. The injector rises, inches from my skin.

Before I can breathe, the world detonates around me.

A shadow drops from above, landing with bone-crushing force on the agent holding me. The impact sends him sprawling, the injector clattering across the stones.

The other agent shouts, baton raised, but the figure moves faster than sight. A twist, a strike, and the baton flies from his hand. A kick sweeps his legs out, slamming him against the wall.

It's over in seconds. Two Dominion enforcers, trained and armed, lie groaning on the ground—disarmed, dazed, but alive. Non-lethal. Deliberate.

And standing over them is the stranger.

He's taller than I expected, lean but taut with coiled strength. His movements are precise, efficient, every motion calculated. A hood shadows half his face, but what I can see is all angles—sharp jaw, cheekbones cut like stone.

And then there's the tattoo.

A raven sprawls across the side of his neck, black wings inked in intricate detail, its beak poised as if mid-cry. In the half-light, the feathers seem to shift, almost alive.

But it's his eyes that catch me most. They're pale, storm lit gray, like lightning caught behind glass. Cold. Unreadable.

He turns that gaze on me, and I freeze.

"Elia Dareth," he says.

My name.

My knees nearly give out. "How—how do you know who I am?"

He doesn't answer. He glances once at the agents on the ground, then back to me.

"You're not safe anymore," he says, voice low, controlled. "Come with me if you want to survive the night."

I stumble back a step, shaking my head. "I—I don't even know you."

His expression doesn't change. "You don't need to."

The agents groan, shifting. One is already reaching for his comm-link. Drones will be here within minutes.

He leans in, voice edged with urgency, as if the air itself has turned tight around us. "They won't stop now. They know what you are."

My heart thunders. Everything in me screams not to trust him—he's dangerous, a rebel, a ghost from the shadows with a raven etched into his skin.

But the Dominion agents on the ground are more dangerous.

And if I stay, I'll be dragged away, injected, erased.

The stranger extends his hand. His palm is steady, sure, waiting.

For one dizzy heartbeat, all I see is his hand—steady, waiting, impossible to ignore.

My breath shakes. My aunt's voice echoes in my head: *Keep your head down. Don't draw attention. Survive.*

But I can't survive this alone.

I grip his hand.

And we run.

The alley twists into darkness, our footsteps pounding in sync. The stranger leads with unnerving precision, weaving through backstreets I didn't know existed. He weaves through the city as if he was born in its veins—under rusted pipes, over shattered fences, always three steps ahead.

Behind us, the thrum of drones rises, blue light flashing. Shouts echo as more agents converge.

"Faster," he snaps, pulling me through a narrow passage. His grip is iron but not cruel, anchoring me as the chaos closes in.

My lungs burn, but I keep pace. The Mark on my wrist pulses hot, like it senses the danger—or maybe the choice I've just made.

We burst onto a wider street, patrol lights sweeping. The stranger swears under his breath, then jerks me into another alley. He presses me against the wall, body taut, as a drone sweeps past above us.

I hold my breath, heart hammering against his arm. His storm-gray eyes flick up, calculating, until the light fades.

Then he pulls back, scanning me briefly. "You need to learn how to move quieter."

I bristle, but before I can snap back, he's already moving again.

Minutes blur into an endless rush of shadows and silence. Finally, we reach a hidden stairwell behind a half-collapsed tower. He pushes the rusted door open, gestures me inside.

The stairwell smells of dust and smoke. My chest heaves as I lean against the wall, finally able to breathe.

The stranger closes the door behind us, locking the world out. For a moment, only the sound of our breaths fills the silence.

I swallow hard. "Who are you?"

He studies me, unreadable. The raven on his neck shifts as he tilts his head.

"That doesn't matter yet," he says. "What matters is this: the Dominion has marked you, and they won't stop. Tonight was only the beginning."

My stomach knots. "Why me?"

A flicker passes through his eyes—something sharp, but gone before I can name it.

"Because you're Crimson," he says simply. "And Crimson is more than they want you to believe."

The words send a shiver down my spine.

I remember the message in ash, the soot-scrawled letters: **CRIMSON IS A KEY, NOT A CURSE.**

And now this stranger, with his storm light eyes is standing before me, confirming it.

Dangerous. Untrustworthy. Yet… maybe the only one who has answers.

He steps closer, lowering his voice. "You need to decide, Elia. Stay, and the Dominion will take you. Or come with me, and maybe you'll live long enough to learn the truth."

I stare at him, my chest tight, every instinct screaming both yes and no.

"Why should I trust you?" I whisper.

His answer is blunt, almost cruel: "You shouldn't. But right now? You've got no other choice."

His hand extends again, palm steady, waiting.

I hesitate—one heartbeat, two. Then I take it.

And step into the unknown.

Chapter 5

Forest of Secrets

The first thing that hits me is the smell.
Not the sterile tang of Dominion scrubber vents or
the metallic hum of city air, but something raw—
damp earth, smoke, pine sap clinging thick to the
back of my throat.

The second thing I notice is the roof. Rough timber
beams, cracked and blackened as if fire once licked
across them. Light seeps through gaps where bark
hasn't been stripped, the forest pressing close enough
to feel alive around me.

I bolt upright.

The pallet beneath me creaks, straw poking through
thin fabric. The walls are uneven planks reinforced
with scavenged metal. No Dominion insignia. No
monitors. No drone ports.

This isn't New Virelia.

I'm in the forest.

Panic spikes. My last clear memory is *him*—storm-
gray eyes in the alley, his hand outstretched, pulling
me into shadows. After that, nothing but blur:
running, a stairwell, the pulse of my Mark like a
second heartbeat.

Now I'm here.
Captured—or worse.

The door groans open before I can move. Two figures enter—rough clothes, scavenged armor, weapons slung with casual precision. Their gazes land on me like weights, cold and assessing.

"She's awake," one mutters.

The other doesn't reply. He just jerks his chin toward the door.

Then he steps in.

He looks exactly as he did in the alley: hood shadowing half his face, raven tattoo stark against his neck, movements sharp as if carved by intent. But here, outside the Dominion's gray walls, he seems… different. Less a shadow, more solid, though no less unreadable.

My breath catches. "Where am I?"

"Off-grid," he says flatly. "A safehouse."

My chest tightens. "Safe? You dragged me out here without my consent. I didn't ask for this."

"You'd be dead if I'd left you." His tone doesn't rise, doesn't falter. Just fact.

I clench my fists, nails biting into my palms. "So now what? I'm your prisoner?"

"You're alive."

The way he says it chills me more than any threat. But there's something under the words too—something I can't name. Regret, maybe. Or recognition.

They lead me outside—not roughly, but with the unmistakable posture of guards.

The air hits me like a blow. The forest stretches in every direction, scarred and wild. Trees tower blackened at the edges, their bark charred from old fires. Between them, rebel structures rise—tents patched from Dominion tarps, huts pieced together with scrap. Smoke curls from a central pit, the scent of ash heavy.

Dozens of eyes turn as I step into the clearing. Men and women, some barely older than me, others weathered, all marked by the same tension: suspicion.

"She's Crimson," someone mutters.
Another spits into the dirt. "And flagged."
A third voice, lower, uneasy: "Better the Forge decide than Lucien's blade."

The air tightens. I feel their distrust like claws scraping my skin.

The raven-marked man doesn't flinch. He simply keeps walking, and I follow—because the alternative is freezing under the weight of so many stares.

We stop at the largest structure—if "largest" means little more than a reinforced shack braced against a blackened oak. Inside, the air is dim, lit only by a lantern's flicker.

A man stands behind a table strewn with maps and scavenged tech. His hair is silver at the temples, his build solid, his expression a storm.

Lucien.

Even without introduction, I know. The way the room bends around his presence makes it obvious.

His gaze cuts over me like a blade. "This is the anomaly?"

The raven-marked man nods once. "Elia Dareth."

Lucien's mouth tightens. "You shouldn't have brought her."

"She wouldn't have survived the night."

"Not our concern." His voice is steel. "Crimsons are bad enough. But a flagged Crimson? That's death— hers, and anyone dumb enough to stand close."

Heat rushes to my face. "I didn't ask to be Crimson."

Lucien's eyes narrow, like I've confirmed some unspoken flaw. "And that's why you can't stay. Dominion will track her here. She'll lead them right to us."

For a moment, silence hangs heavy.

The raven-marked man—Cassian, I remember now—doesn't argue. He just watches me with that storm-light gaze.

Finally, Lucien snaps, "Keep her contained until I decide."

He turns back to his maps—but this time I notice the edges of the papers aren't new. They're scorched, water-stained, corners held together with trembling hands. His left sleeve rides up as he moves, revealing a Dominion officer's brand seared faintly into his forearm. The mark's been burned over, but not erased.

For an instant, something flickers behind his cold restraint—a fracture, gone as quickly as it comes.

Cassian's jaw tightens, but his voice stays low. "You always said we fight for the ones they burn."

Lucien's reply is sharp. "And I intend to. That's why sentiment kills faster than bullets. Don't mistake survival for cruelty."

He doesn't raise his voice, but the words feel like orders carved from grief.

They don't lock me up. Not exactly.

But when Cassian leads me back to the smaller hut, two guards position themselves outside. Inside, the

pallet waits, rough and cold. No chains, no cuffs—
but the message is clear.

I'm not trusted.

He stands in the doorway for a moment before
leaving. His eyes flick over the room, then back to
me.

"You'll stay put," he says quietly.

"Until Lucien decides if I'm worth keeping alive?"

His expression doesn't change, but the corner of his
mouth twitches like it might. "Something like that."

I cross my arms. "You always this charming?"

For the first time, there's the ghost of a smile—small,
reluctant, gone in an instant. "Only with people who
threaten to bite."

It shouldn't make my chest tighten, but it does.
Something in his tone isn't mockery; it's fatigue,
almost gentleness disguised as armor.

He starts to leave, then pauses with his hand on the
doorframe. "You said you didn't ask for this. Neither
did I."
Then he's gone.

The words linger longer than they should.

I sit on the edge of the bed, arms wrapped tight around myself. Anger churns under the fear, a restless storm. I want to scream at them, demand answers, claw my way back to the city just to prove I can't be caged.

But one look at the forest outside silences me.

The trees rise tall and dark, branches clawing at the sky. Beyond them, I hear the faint hum of drones patrolling the perimeter, their lights flashing through the haze. The Dominion's reach stretches even here.

Running isn't an option. Not without being caught— or worse.

I'm trapped between enemies I know and enemies I don't.

Hours later, Cassian returns.

He leans against the doorframe, arms crossed. His eyes catch mine, and something in my chest jolts again.

"You've made quite an impression," he says dryly.

I glare. "Your people hate me."

"They don't hate you. They fear you."

The words sting more than I expect. "Because I'm Crimson."

"Because you're an anomaly."

I frown. "What does that even mean?"

He steps inside, movements precise. "The Dominion's predictions are absolute. Every Mark follows their patterns—until now. You don't fit. Your scans don't align. That makes you unpredictable."

"Unpredictable? That doesn't have to mean dangerous."

"To them, it does." His eyes soften, barely. "And maybe they're not wrong."

My pulse spikes. "You don't even know me."

"I know enough." His gaze sharpens, storm-light eyes cutting through me. "They mark who they fear most. And yours burns redder than any we've seen."

The words settle heavy in the air, more riddle than answer.

"What does that mean?" I whisper.

He doesn't explain. He just turns, hand on the doorframe. "Get some rest. You'll need it."

But he hesitates—just long enough for me to catch the way his fingers tense, like he wants to say something else. The lamplight cuts across his face, silver and shadow.

"Why did you really save me?" I ask softly.

He exhales. Not quite a sigh. "Because for a second, when I saw you in that alley, I thought I was seeing myself."

Then he leaves.

The night stretches long. Every creak of the forest sets my nerves on edge. I keep thinking of Lucien's eyes—cold, calculating, but not empty. And Cassian's, which weren't cold at all. Just guarded.

I want to run. I want to throw myself into the trees, push past the drones, find my way back to the city.

But I remember the injector glinting in the agent's hand. The way they said *flagged subject* like it was already a death sentence.

Safe doesn't exist—not with the Dominion, not with rebels, maybe not even with me.

At some point, silence swallows the camp. The guards outside shift, their voices fading.

I wander the hut restlessly, fingers brushing over splintered wood, scavenged blankets, a cracked metal basin leaning in the corner. I lift it, meaning to move it aside.

Then I freeze.

The inside gleams faintly, warped but reflective enough to catch my face.

And my wrist.

The Crimson Mark pulses faintly in the mirror, brighter than I've ever seen. Not constant—like a heartbeat, alive beneath my skin.

For a moment, I can't breathe.

It's not just ink. Not just a designation.

It's something more.

Alive. Beating. Waiting.

I set the basin down, hands shaking, the echo of Cassian's words searing through me:
They mark who they fear the most. Yours burns redder than any we've seen.

And for the first time, I wonder if my Mark is not just a curse—
but the beginning of something else.

Chapter 6

Classified Blood

The rebels call it the Hollow.
Whisper it, almost like the name itself might break.

No maps mark it, no Dominion drones pierce its
canopy. The forest here grows twisted—blackened
trunks leaning at strange angles, branches like scarred
bones clawing at the sky. Old fires left their marks
long ago, and yet life presses through: moss softening
the ash, vines clawing stubbornly up fractured bark.

Safe? Not even close. But hidden—yes.
And hidden, in Dominion territory, is the closest
thing to freedom.

On my second day in the Hollow, he comes for me.

"You need to understand why you're here," he says,
tone clipped as always. His storm-gray eyes flicker
once to my wrist where my Crimson Mark glows
faintly, then back to my face. "There are answers. Or
at least… explanations."

I don't trust him, not entirely. But I follow—because
what choice do I have?

He leads me to a low structure near the forest's edge,
its roof patched with scavenged Dominion plating.
Inside, lanterns cast soft light over shelves upon
shelves of scrolls, books, even crumbling paper—
things I thought the Dominion had burned out of

existence. The air smells of smoke and ink, old parchment preserved with desperate care.

A man hunches over the table at the center. His hair is iron gray though his face is not yet old, his hands stained with ink and burn scars that creep up his wrists like vines. He glances up, eyes sharp behind wire spectacles.

"Ansel," Cassian says simply. "She needs the history."

Ansel studies me for a long moment, gaze weighing more than measuring. Then he motions to the bench opposite.

"Sit, child," he says, voice steady as old wood, though his eyes look sharp enough to cut. "If you carry Crimson, you carry questions. Better they be answered before they eat you alive."

He begins not with my parents, not with the Dominion, but with a story.

But before he can unroll the first parchment, something on the cluttered side table catches my eye. At first it looks like scrap—shards of glass, a twisted piece of metal, a small blackened flake the size of a fingernail.

For no reason I can name, my hand moves without permission. I pick it up.

It warms almost instantly, as that thing in the market did—only smaller, more deliberate. Ember-red letters flare across the surface for a single heartbeat, then collapse into gray ash that sifts through my fingers like dust. The words are gone, but the memory of them lives like a brand behind my eyes.

Ansel watches me, and for a second his expression softens into something like pity. "You remember the market, then."

I look at him. "You made that?" My voice is small.

He nods without ceremony. "Once, yes. Rebellion tech. But the design was stolen—from the Dominion archives." His mouth twists slightly. "From me."

My stomach turns. "You worked for them?"

"Once," he says, and something in the word sounds fractured. "Before the Hollow. Before I understood what my research would become."

He lifts one of his burned hands. "I built the first generation of their scanners. Thought I was mapping health anomalies. Turns out I was building the cages they'd brand into children."

The confession hangs heavy in the dim air.

"They called it Predictive Science," he says, almost to himself. "I called it salvation. I was wrong."

He straightens, pushing away the ghost of memory. "Now I use what I know to dismantle what I built."

He draws a deep breath, steadying. "Ash-messages are fragments of the same code—rewritten to vanish before their eyes. Hope rewritten from the bones of surveillance."

My breath stumbles. The market boy, the vendor's hand brushing mine, the words on my skin—the memory snaps into place. It wasn't coincidence. It was intention.

"They're designed to erase before the Dominion can file them," Ansel continues. "Transient signals. Whispered instructions. Hope in a flake." He taps the table where the gray ash dust clings. "We use them sparingly. Too many and the scanners catch patterns. Too few and the message dies before it finds a hand."

My fingers curl tight around the empty space where the ash was. "So it was you. You were watching me."

"We watch the threads where the Dominion frays," Ansel says quietly. "We look for places where fear can be unpicked. Sometimes we nudge. Sometimes we wait. You were visible, child. Not because you asked to be, but because you were a seam worth pulling."

He pulls a faded Dominion dossier across the table. The seal is cracked, the pages yellowing. He taps a line of text.

"Two centuries ago," he says, "the Marks were science, not prophecy. Dominion researchers developed biometric algorithms—ways to map a child's bloodline, neural patterns, even micro-expressions. They believed they could predict violent outcomes before they happened. The Marks were meant to save lives. A warning, nothing more."

I frown. "So they were... supposed to help?"

"In theory," Ansel says. "It should've been a guide. Instead, it snapped into a leash. Children branded before they even grew into themselves. And the Dominion discovered fear was the strongest leash of all."

He points to the dossier's table, where cold numbers sit beside colder declarations. "Look at this. Crimson was high-risk, yes, but never certain."

I lean closer. The words swim before me: *Predictive model output: 82% probability of violent end before 19.* Eighty-two. Not a hundred. Not absolute. Not doomed.

My breath catches.

"They never told us that. Not once. Not ever."

"Of course not," Ansel says softly. "Control thrives on certainty. If you believe you're doomed, you don't fight. You accept."

My chest tightens. Every moment of my life since thirteen—the way neighbors turned cold, the way teachers avoided my gaze, the way my aunt pressed my sleeves lower—it was all built on a Dominion lie.

Ansel's eyes darken. "Because the Dominion hunts them. Fear justifies the purge. Crimson is not death by nature—it is death by design."

The words burn hotter than fire.

All the propaganda screens, the warnings, the whispers that Crimson means instability, Crimson means danger—all of it twisting truth until we believed we were cursed.

I think of Dax. Gone after his Recount. Everyone whispered unstable, dangerous, doomed. But if Ansel is right... maybe he wasn't doomed at all. Maybe he was taken.

My throat aches. "They lied to us."

"They always lie," Ansel murmurs. "I should know— I used to write the scripts they broadcast."

He rises, crossing to a shelf where the oldest scrolls lie bundled in worn leather. Carefully, he draws one free, unrolling it across the table. The parchment is brittle, but the ink still lingers, black strokes curling into symbols I don't recognize.

"These are older than the Dominion," Ansel says. "From before the empire consolidated its grip. Ancient texts, passed down in fragments."

He traces a finger along the symbols. "They speak of a Crimson Seed. One marked in red whose blood defies prediction. A spark, they say, to break the algorithm's chain. To light rebellion like dry tinder."

The words strike me like a blow.

I recoil. "No. That's... that's just another prophecy. A story to make people hope."

"Maybe," Ansel says calmly. "But every rebellion begins with a story."

I shake my head. "You talk like you believe it."

His smile is faint, weary. "Belief built empires. Maybe it can break one too."

"I'm not anyone's prophecy. I'm not. I'm just trying to breathe, to stay alive."

For the first time, Ansel looks directly at me—not as a relic, not as a scholar, but as a man who's seen the inside of both cages: the Dominion's and his own guilt.

"That's what they all say," he murmurs. "Until the algorithm fails to predict them."

The words linger, heavy and unsettling.

Later that night, when the camp quiets and most rebels retreat to their fires, I step outside, thoughts churning too loudly for sleep. The forest air is damp, moss sharp after rain.

And the man with the raven tattoo is there.

He leans against a blackened tree, arms crossed, storm-light eyes scanning the shadows. The raven tattoo on his neck gleams faintly in the firelight.

"You vanished after Ansel's lesson," he says without looking at me.

"I needed air," I mutter.

He finally turns his gaze on me. That storm-gray stare strips me bare. "And what do you think now? Still believe the Dominion's story of what you are?"

"I don't know what I believe. But I know I don't trust you."

Something flickers in his eyes—amusement, maybe. "Good. Trust? That's what'll get you killed."

We stand in silence, the forest whispering around us. I can't take it anymore.

"Who are you?" The words crack sharper than I mean. "You appear out of nowhere, you save me, you drag me into this camp where everyone looks at me like I'm a disease. You know my name, my Mark, things I've never told anyone. And I don't even know what to call you."

For a moment, I think he won't answer. Then, slowly, he steps closer, shadows brushing his face.

"My name is Cassian."

The word is low, steady, like stone dropping into water.

It reverberates through me. Finally, the shadow has a name.

"Cassian," I repeat softly.

He inclines his head once, the raven tattoo flexing with the movement. "Now you know."

He starts to turn away, but something keeps me rooted. "Why do you care what I believe?"

He pauses—half in shadow, half in the amber glow of the dying fire. For a heartbeat, he looks younger. Tired, but human.
"Because belief is what kept me alive once," he says. His voice lowers. "And maybe I wanted to see if it could keep someone else."

For reasons I can't explain, the air shifts between us. The firelight flickers across his face—silver on scar, light on storm.
And when he looks at me again, it's not suspicion in his eyes this time. It's recognition.

It's gone in a breath, swallowed by the dark.

When I return to the hut, my mind refuses to quiet. I sink onto the straw pallet, staring at the cracked basin in the corner—the makeshift mirror I found before.

Slowly, I lift it.

My reflection stares back, pale and exhausted. But it's the Mark that draws me.

Crimson. Pulsing faintly in the dim light. Not constant. Not dead.

Alive. Breathing under my skin, like it has a mind of its own.

I set the basin down, trembling, Ansel's words echoing like thunder:
That's what they all say—until the algorithm fails to predict them.

And for the first time, I wonder if I am more than the Dominion's curse.

Maybe I am the anomaly.
Maybe I am the failure in their chain.

And if that's true—then everything I thought about survival is about to change.

Chapter 7

Beneath the Broken Code

The Hollow breathes differently at night.
In the day, it feels like a scar—stitched together from
scavenged wood and Dominion scrap. But when the
fires burn low and the watchmen pace with rifles
across their shoulders, the air hums with something
else. Not safety. Not peace. Something closer to…
possibility.

That's when Cassian finds me.

"Ansel isn't the only one with answers," he says.
"Come."

He doesn't wait to see if I follow. He never does. And
still—I go. Because whenever he says *come*, the
alternative feels like standing still in quicksand.

We cut across the clearing to a hut sunk low into the
ground, more bunker than shelter. Its door is
reinforced steel, half-buried in earth, a rebel sigil
smeared across it in soot. Cassian raps twice. Sharp.
The door groans open.

Inside, the light is wrong—harsh and electric instead
of warm lantern glow. Dominion tech, scavenged and
reworked. Floodlamps. Cables crawling over the dirt
floor. Screens flickering with fractured images.
Generators hum like they're on their last breath.

At least six people work here. One hunched over a cracked Dominion keyboard. Another bent close to a circuit board, sparks popping as she solders. The air tastes of ozone and burnt metal.

A woman glances up, eyes rimmed red from lack of sleep. Her scowl is instant when she sees me. "You brought her here?"

"She needs to see," Cassian says. Simple. Unshaken.

The woman mutters but turns back to her screen.

I hover near the door, every instinct screaming to leave. Suspicion is thicker down here—like every glance is calculating the cost of letting me breathe their air.

Cassian gestures at the central console. "This is where the Dominion's leash gets cut."

On the monitor glows a schematic. An implant. My stomach flips. The same model embedded in my wrist since childhood. Rebel shorthand crawls around the edges: *tracking beacon neutralized, biometric lock cracked, log corruption possible.*

A wiry man yanks off his headset, steady hands tapping the keys like they're an extension of him. "Every citizen's got one," he says. "Every movement, every heartbeat—Dominion code watches it all. They call it security. Truth? It's surveillance in your blood."

He flicks a switch. A side screen flares, streams of numbers racing in green and white. "We jam the trackers, reroute the signals. That's why the Hollow stays invisible. But…" He cuts a look at Cassian. "The anomaly should see her file."

My chest tightens. "My file?"

He pulls it up. My name screams at the top:
DARETH, ELIA. CRIMSON. FLAGGED.
Line after line records me: my pulse during Recount, biometrics in the square, the moment the scanner caught my Mark. My life compressed into code. Numbers pretending to be me.

I can barely breathe.

"Here," the man mutters, stabbing a finger at a section of data. "This is where she breaks it."

I lean closer. The lines flow clean and precise—until they don't. Static tears through them. Bursts of unreadable symbols scatter across the screen like sparks from a burning wire.

"Error logs," the woman says, reluctant but watching anyway. "Her implant's been glitching since her Marking. Random corruption. Dominion hardware doesn't glitch like this."

My throat dries. "So… what does it mean?"

Cassian's voice is low. Flat. "It means their algorithm can't pin you down."

The room goes colder.

The archivist's words echo back: *Crimson Seed.* A
bloodline that defies prediction.
But here it isn't prophecy. It's Dominion code
breaking.

The strongest system in the world—cracking open on
me.

Every set of eyes is on me now. Some curious. Some
afraid. Some sharp, already measuring how to use me.

Something in me snaps.

"You talk like I'm not even a person," I burst out,
voice rough. "Like I'm some weapon the Dominion
forged wrong. I didn't ask for this. I didn't ask to be
Crimson, or flagged, or broken in your code. I'm a
girl. I just want to survive."

Silence. The machines buzz. The monitors flicker. But
the people hold their breath.

Cassian doesn't.

He steps forward, shadows carving across his face.
His storm-gray eyes find mine, steady as steel.

"Weapons don't choose what they destroy," he says.
Quiet. Merciless. "But they can choose where they
aim."

The words cut deep. I want to spit them back, to scream. But the worst part is—I don't know if he's wrong.

Because if the Dominion fears me… if their system can't cage me… maybe I am dangerous.
And if I am—what then?

My vision tunnels. The hum swells until it's a single hard note. I realize I'm breathing too fast; the room tilts.

"Hey." The word is barely above a whisper.

Cassian is closer than I thought—close enough that the ozone on his jacket mingles with smoke and rain. He doesn't touch me, not at first. He only angles his body so I'm shielded from the screens, from their eyes.

"Breathe." The command is soft this time. Not an order. A hand hovers in the space between us, waiting, not presuming. "In four. Hold. Out four."

I match him because I don't know what else to do. Air in. Hold. Out.
Our breaths find the same rhythm—an accidental sync. The hum quiets.

His hand drifts, finally, to the back of my forearm. Barely there. Warm through the ash-dust on my skin. Not claiming. Just… steady.

"Better," he murmurs. The word is for me alone.

Later, when Cassian leaves me at the hut, I can't sleep. My pulse hammers, my thoughts tangling with prophecy and corrupted code. Their stares burned into my skin.

I slip outside. The night is damp, cool, leaves dripping under a thin moon.

I sink onto a fallen log, palms pressed to my knees.
Memories rise, jagged and uninvited.
My mother, the night before she vanished, cupping my face with trembling hands: *You are more than their data.*
My father, gripping my wrist where the Mark still burned raw: *Don't let them write your story for you.*

I buried those words years ago. Too afraid to hope. Too afraid to believe.
But tonight, they won't stay buried.

Footsteps scuff the leaf litter behind me. I don't startle; somehow I already know.

Cassian stops a few paces away, the moon catching in his eyes. He holds out a battered canteen.

"You forgot this," he says.

"I never had it."

A corner of his mouth lifts—almost. "Then I'm early."

I take the canteen. Our fingers brush. The contact is nothing and everything, a spark finding dry tinder.

He doesn't move to sit. Doesn't crowd the quiet he's made.

"You think I'm a weapon," I say, the words tasting like iron.

"I think you're a choice," he answers. "And choices scare empires."

"Do they scare you?"

His jaw tightens. For a heartbeat, the storm in him looks almost human. "Yes."

The truth hangs between us, clean and dangerous. He steps back, as if he's said too much.

"Breathe," he says again, softer. "In four. Hold. Out four."

Then he's gone—lost to the trees, the way he always is.

I drink the water. It's warm metal and relief. I watch the darkness until it looks less like a wall and more like a path.

What if Ansel's right?
What if Cassian's right?
What if different isn't a curse?
What if different is the point?

The thought terrifies me. But beneath the terror, something sparks—fragile, trembling, stubborn.

Hope.

Chapter 8

Cassian's Mission

The Hollow never really sleeps. But it does fall quiet. By night, the forest hums with insects, drones sweep the perimeter in slow arcs, and the rebels keep to murmurs. Fires gutter low, casting long shadows that crawl like skeletal fingers across the ground.

I should be asleep, buried under the scratchy blanket in the drafty hut they gave me. But my mind won't stop.
Ansel's words echo: *Crimson is not a curse, it is a key.*
The lab's screens flicker behind my eyes. My parents' voices whisper in memory. The Mark on my wrist pulses faintly—alive, insistent.

So I walk.

The Hollow was carved out of old Dominion defenses—burned decades ago. Ruins still stand at the edges: crumbled towers, melted steel, vines dragging them back into the earth. It's quieter here, away from the rebels' campfires. I prefer it.

That's where I see Cassian.

He sits on the broken wall, hood shoved back, raven tattoo catching pale moonlight. A knife twirls in his hand, blade flashing with each spin. He doesn't look up when I approach. Doesn't need to. He always knows.

"You never sleep, do you?" I ask. My voice tries for casual and misses.

"Sleep's a luxury," he answers, still watching the knife. "One I can't afford."

I lower myself onto the stone, not too close. For a while, we just listen. The forest breathes. The silence between us is sharp—but not unbearable.

"You were watching me," I say finally.

His eyes flick to mine—storm-gray, unreadable. "Always."

The word twists something in my chest. I hate it. Hate that he makes me feel anything but suspicion.

"Why?"

The knife stops spinning. He slides it back into its sheath. "Because you're dangerous."

The words sting. I expected them. Still, they cut. "You sound just like them."

"No." His voice is quiet, steady. "They fear what they don't understand. I watch because I need to."

And for the first time, his armor shifts. Shoulders drop, jaw unclenches. The Cassian I know—sharp edges, ruthless precision—cracks. And there's something else beneath.

"Elia." My name leaves him softer this time. Not flat. Almost… human.

The sound of it catches me off guard. It shouldn't feel like anything, but it does. Like hearing your name for the first time after being called everything else.

"There's something you don't know," he says carefully. "If I keep it, it destroys us both."

My pulse spikes. "What do you mean?"

His gaze lifts, and the storm inside finally breaks.

"My orders," he says. "The night I pulled you from the Dominion. Lucien gave me the mission himself."

The pit opens in my stomach. I know what's coming before he says it.

"If you destabilized. If the anomaly grew too dangerous. If you were more risk than asset…" His voice hardens. "I was to end you. Quiet. Clean."

The ground tilts. My breath vanishes.
Then fury floods in.

"You—" My voice shatters like glass. "You were supposed to kill me?"

Cassian doesn't move. Doesn't flinch. He takes it like a blow.

I'm on my feet, grabbing the nearest thing—an empty glass bottle from the mess tents—and I hurl it. It smashes against the wall near his head, shards scattering in the moonlight.

"You're just like them!" My throat rips with the scream. "You think my life is a line of code to delete. A threat to erase. A problem to solve. I'm not a weapon. I'm not a prophecy. I'm a girl who's had everything ripped away, and you—" My voice breaks. "You were supposed to be different."

For the first time, Cassian looks raw. Not broken. But stripped.

"I didn't do it," he says, hoarse. "I was meant to— and I didn't. Do you know what that means?"

He stands, closing the space between us even as I want to shove him back.

"I haven't reported you since that night," he says. "Every day I delay, I betray Lucien. Betray the rebellion. I've already chosen, Elia. I chose you."

Tears sting. My head shakes. "You chose hesitation. That's not the same as choosing me."

His jaw clenches. "Maybe not. But hesitation is more than anyone else would've given you."

The words hang heavy.

I want to hate him. Want to drive my fists into his chest, scream until the forest swallows me whole. But beneath the fury, something curls tighter, dangerous. Because he's right.
If it had been Lucien—or anyone else—I wouldn't still be breathing.

The silence stretches brittle. The Hollow glows faint behind us, embers like tired stars.

Cassian drops his gaze. And suddenly he doesn't look like the storm-forged soldier, the shadow marked by a raven. He just looks tired.

"I won't ask forgiveness," he says softly. "But I will tell you this: they don't own your life. Not the Dominion. Not Lucien. Not me."

He turns to leave. The movement catches the moonlight across his jaw, across the scar by his temple. For the first time, I notice his hands shaking—barely, but there. The knife at his hip glints, untouched.

Something in me softens against my will.

"Cassian." The word slips out before I can stop it.

He pauses.

I take a step forward, voice low. "Why me? Why didn't you just follow orders?"

He exhales, slow. When he speaks, it's quieter than I've ever heard him.

"Because when you looked at me that night—in the alley—you didn't look afraid. You looked alive."

His eyes meet mine then, and the world tilts again—but differently this time. The night folds closer, like the forest itself is holding its breath.

"I thought I'd forgotten what that looked like," he adds.

I can't answer. My chest is a battlefield—rage and something else clawing for ground.

He steps back, the distance between us turning heavy again. "Sleep, Elia. Tomorrow, we move."

He starts to go.

"Next time," I whisper, "don't hesitate."

He freezes. The moonlight cuts sharp across his face.

"I won't," he says—and for a moment, his voice isn't warning or promise. It's both.

The words taste of iron. Of truth. Of something neither of us are ready to name.
And under the fractured moon, the crack between us splits wider—
not apart,
but open.

Chapter 9

The Raven's Orders

The Hollow feels different after betrayal.

Rebels still haul water, mend gear, bank fires. Same routines. But the air tastes sharper now, like metal on my tongue. Like a blade against my throat. Every glance lingers too long. Every whisper sounds like it's about me.
Maybe it is.

Cassian's confession gnaws like teeth: *My orders were to end you.* He said it like a soldier reporting facts, not a man asking forgiveness. That's what makes it worse.

I haven't spoken to him since. Haven't even looked at him unless I can't avoid it. But tonight, the fury bubbling in me won't stay caged.

I find him at the Hollow's edge, perched against the skeleton of a charred tree overlooking the valley. Fog presses heavy, moonlight barely cutting through. His hood hides most of his face, but I'd know him anywhere—the rigid posture, the stillness like he was carved from stone.

"You're getting better at walking without sound," he says without turning.

My skin prickles. He always notices.

"Don't change the subject," I snap.

His head tilts slightly, but he doesn't face me. "What subject?"

I step closer, fists clenched. "You lied. You dragged me here, told me I wasn't safe—while carrying orders to kill me."

Finally, he lifts his gaze. Storm-gray eyes catch the moonlight.

"I didn't lie," he says quietly. "I didn't kill you."

"That's not the same thing."

Silence swells between us. The forest fills it—the creak of branches, the drone hum far off at the perimeter.

Then Cassian exhales, like something cracking inside him. "You deserve the truth. All of it."

He gestures toward the valley, where faint Dominion lights flicker on the horizon. "You know what they are. What they've done. But not what we fight for."

I cross my arms. My voice is sharp. "Enlighten me."

His eyes stay on the horizon. "The Dominion's systems were meant for protection. That's what the old records claim. But protection twisted into control. The algorithm doesn't just forecast behavior—it manufactures it. Marks become lives. Green obeys. Amber hides. Blue enforces the Chancellor's rules. Crimson dies. Dominion thrives on the certainty."

His jaw tightens. "The Raven Network exists to end it. To burn their chains."

"The Raven Network," I echo, glancing at the black wings on his neck. Not decoration. A brand.

"We dismantle them piece by piece—archives, servers, every eye they have. One day, their heart."

"And me?" My voice cuts. "Where do I fit? Am I your weapon, your key, or your liability?"

He doesn't flinch. Doesn't soften.
"You don't fit."

The words cut deeper than I expect.

"Your Mark glitches their system," he continues. "Your scans fail. Your implant logs corrupt. You're unreadable. And that makes you..." He holds my gaze. "...a glitch in their chain."

The word sinks heavy. *A glitch.*

"They see you as dangerous because you wreck their certainty," he says. "And the truth? They're right. You are dangerous. To them. To us."

My throat tightens. "To you? Why?"

"Because unpredictability cuts both ways. If their system can't read you, neither can we. You could be a Trojan horse. A trigger waiting. One spark, and everything we've built burns."

I shake my head, fierce. "I'm not your enemy."

"Maybe not," Cassian says. "But you could be. And that's enough."

Anger spikes hot. "So to everyone—Dominion, rebels—I'm just a threat."

His expression flickers. Softer. Almost pained. "To me, you're more than that."

The words fall between us, fragile as glass.

I stare at him, searching. And for once, he looks less like the storm-forged soldier, more like a man pulled in two.

"My loyalty is to the Network," he says, voice low. "To my brother. To the cause. But from the night I pulled you from Dominion hands—I broke that loyalty. Every day I don't report you is treason."

His hands curl into fists. "And I don't regret it."

The night presses close. My chest aches with anger, fear, and something I refuse to name.

Cassian turns back toward the valley. Dominion lights pulse faint, distant. His voice hardens again.

"They fear you because they can't predict you."
Then his eyes cut to mine.
"But so do we. That makes you dangerous to everyone."

The words shatter something inside me.

We stand in silence, the forest holding its breath.

And I realize: it doesn't matter what I want. To both sides, I'll never be just Elia. I'll always be the anomaly. The glitch. The Crimson Seed.

Whatever they decide I am.

Unless I decide first.

Behind us, faint voices drift from the Hollow—sharp, hushed, carrying on the night air.

"She's Crimson. The Dominion already marked her." "Then let the Forge prove it," another snaps back.

The words cut colder than the fog. I don't know what the Forge is, but the way they spit it like a sentence makes my skin crawl.

Chapter 10

Trial by Flame

The Hollow wakes me before dawn.

Drums.
Low and steady, thudding through the scarred forest
like a second heartbeat. The sound rattles my hut,
makes the jars on the shelf tremble. Outside, voices
rise—rebels gathering, restless.

I sit up, chest pounding. I already know.
They've decided.

Cassian waits at the door. Hood pushed back, eyes
storm-gray and unreadable. He doesn't soften it,
doesn't pretend. Just says:
"Lucien called for you."

The clearing looks different this morning.
Rebels stand in a wide circle around a pit of
blackened stone, their faces harsh in the cold light.
Lucien waits at the center—broad shoulders, dark
hair, presence sharp as fire. Where Cassian carries
storms in silence, Lucien burns. Charisma,
ruthlessness, calculation in every glance.

When his eyes lock on me, they narrow. Assessment.
Judgment.

"Crimson," he calls, his voice steel. "You've hidden in
the Hollow. No longer. The Dominion hunts you.

And until I know whether you're a danger or a weapon, you are a liability."

Murmurs ripple through the circle. Some nod. Others glance uneasily at Cassian.

Lucien raises a hand. Silence drops like a blade. "So we test you. In the Forge."

The Forge is older than the rebellion. A Dominion bunker left to rot, half-collapsed into the earth. The rebels twisted it into something else—a chamber of trials.

Cassian leads me down slick steps, moss thick underfoot. Torches burn in iron brackets, smoke curling black against stone. The deeper we go, the heavier the air presses—until the tunnel yawns into a chamber alive with fire.

At the center: a ring of scorched steel. Chains dangle from hooks in the ceiling. Metal doors line the walls, faintly humming, waiting.

Lucien steps inside. His voice echoes off stone. "This is not a fight of fists. This is a trial by flame. We see what survives when everything else burns."

My stomach twists.
I whisper to Cassian, "And if I refuse?"

His jaw locks. "Then you're already dead."

But his eyes flicker—just once. Not cold, not cruel.
Something tighter. Guilt, maybe. Fear. I can't tell.

The trial begins with light.

Blinding, white-hot. Then voices—cold,
mechanical—Dominion commands barking through
hidden speakers.
"Subject: Crimson. Flagged. Unstable."

Chains rattle. My arms jerk upward though no hands
touch me. The Forge ripples. Scarred walls shift into
sterile steel, Dominion insignia glowing red.

I know this place. The Recount chambers.

Figures march out of the light—agents in black
helmets, injectors gleaming. Their visors reflect my
terrified face.
One voice intones, flat as glass: "Terminate anomaly."

The needle bites cold against my skin.

Panic erupts. I thrash, wrists tearing against invisible
binds. My pulse thunders. Images slam into me—my
parents before they vanished, Dax laughing before his
Recount, my aunt's tight eyes every time she told me
to hide.

All ending here. All ending in fire.

Something inside me breaks. *No.*

I rip free—not with strength, but with refusal. The bind cracks. I hurl myself at the nearest figure, knocking the injector away. His visor smashes against the floor and bursts into smoke.

The others close in.

Instinct screams: fight harder, claw, destroy. But when I catch the eyes behind one visor—human eyes, wide with fear—I falter.
They look like me.
Not monsters. Just people caught in the machine.

My voice shreds out. "You don't have to do this. You're more than their orders. More than their data."

The figures hesitate. The simulation flickers. Walls ripple like smoke.

A final voice booms: "Crimson cannot be trusted."

I lift my chin, chest heaving. "Maybe not. But I trust me. And I'm still here."

The white light shatters.

I hit my knees in the Forge. The chamber is stone again. No chains. No blood. My body unmarked, but sweat drips down my spine, my heart hammering out of control.

The rebels watch from the edges. Faces shadowed. Some shaken. Some look at me like a weapon. Others—like something else entirely.

Lucien steps forward. Circles me once, a predator measuring prey.

"She didn't break."

His gaze slices to the crowd. "She fought—but not with Dominion violence. She resisted with something rarer. Empathy."

The word lands like ash. Disdain, but respect too.

"She isn't a weapon," Lucien says. His eyes flick sharp to Cassian. "She's a catalyst. And catalysts are more dangerous than blades."

The circle erupts. Murmurs split—hope, fear, both. *Catalyst. Change. Catalyst. Collapse.*

Lucien's hand cuts the noise. His stare pins me like iron.
"You may stay," he declares. "For now. But do not mistake this for mercy. This is strategy. We will use what you are—until you burn us, or burn them."

Then his gaze slams into Cassian. Colder. Sharper. "And you. Don't get attached. She's marked to burn."

The words bite deeper than flame.

Cassian doesn't move, but I see it—the storm locked in his eyes.
The muscle in his jaw tightens; his hands curl against his sides, as if the only thing keeping him still is will alone.

Lucien turns away. The crowd scatters, voices rising again. But Cassian doesn't follow. Not right away.

When he finally steps forward, his voice is low enough for only me.
"I tried to fight it."

I look up, breath unsteady. "Fight what?"

"The order. The Forge. I argued you weren't ready. Lucien doesn't listen to reason—only results." He hesitates, then adds, "I thought I could protect you from it."

The words hit harder than the trial itself. Because under them, I hear something unspoken: *I couldn't.*

"You didn't stop it," I whisper. "You brought me here."

"I know." His voice cracks around the admission. He forces himself to meet my gaze, and for once, he doesn't hide behind orders. "And I'll live with that."

The silence that follows isn't empty. It's alive.

The firelight flickers across his face, and for the first time since I met him, Cassian looks *haunted.* Not by death, but by me.

"I didn't want you to see me like that," I say, the words trembling before I can swallow them back.

He exhales slowly. "I've seen worse things in this war."
A pause.
"But none that made me want to stop it more."

Something sharp twists in my chest. I don't know what to do with it—this strange gravity pulling us together even as the world burns around us.

He glances once toward the upper steps, where Lucien disappeared. "He'll make you a symbol now. That's how he wins people—he turns them into causes."

"And what about you?" I ask. "What do you turn people into?"

He looks at me for a long moment. Then, softly: "Ghosts."

And then he leaves.

But just before he vanishes into the tunnel, he stops—one hand against the wall, shoulders rigid. He doesn't look back, but his voice carries, quiet and raw: "You didn't burn, Elia."
A beat.
"Don't start now."

The chamber hums with dying firelight. Smoke curls around me, warm and bitter.

I survived the Forge.
But the storm between us—that's what will set everything ablaze.

Chapter 11

Static and Silence

The Hollow doesn't give me space to breathe after the Forge.

Barely a day passes before Lucien summons Cassian and three others into his war room. I don't expect to be included—not after being branded a *catalyst*, not a soldier.

But when Cassian emerges, hood low over storm-gray eyes, all he says is:

"You're coming."

And I follow.

The target: a Dominion outpost ten miles east. One of dozens circling the forest like teeth. Not a fortress—just a surveillance hub, its drones mapping every shadow of rebel movement.

"Cutting their eyes out," **Tova** mutters while checking gear. She's wiry, sharp-eyed, and looks like she's been stitched together by sleepless nights. Her dark curls are tied back with torn gauze, and her medpack bulges like it's ready to burst.

"Not glamorous," she says, testing the weight of her pistol before holstering it. "Like scrubbing latrines, only with more chance of dying."

Jules grins too wide, too eager. He can't be more than sixteen, hair a mess of blond tangles, a strip of fabric tied around his wrist where a Mark should be.

"Necessary still matters," he says. "We pull this off, people live."

Tova snorts. "Keep chanting that, kid. Might even start to sound true."

Cassian says nothing. He loads his rifle, precise and silent.

And me? I fumble into scavenged armor that reeks of rust and smoke, trying to keep my hands steady.

When I struggle with the straps, Tova steps over and tightens one with brisk efficiency. "Don't let it hang loose," she says. "A gap's where bullets like to hide." Her tone is dry, but her fingers linger a beat too long, checking the placement. She notices the faint shimmer of my Mark and looks away quickly.
"I've patched up plenty of Crimsons," she mutters. "Most didn't stay patched long."
I can't tell if it's a warning or a confession.

We leave before dawn, a thin line of shadows through black trees. Ash crunches soft underfoot, moss muffles the rest.

Cassian leads. Tova behind him, medpack heavy. Jules drifts near me, whispering questions he shouldn't.
"Is it true you glitched their scanners?" His eyes glitter.
My breath stutters. "Where'd you hear that?"
"Everyone's heard," he says. "Some think you're dangerous. I think you're proof they can be beaten."

Dangerous. Proof. Catalyst. The words echo heavier than my boots.

He walks beside me a while longer, quieter now. "I used to work the relay towers outside New Virelia. Maintenance crew. My job was to clear static from Dominion feeds. I figured if I understood their machines, someday I could break them. Guess I got my wish."

I glance at him. "You were Dominion tech?"
"Barely. My brother still is. He thinks I'm dead." His grin falters for the first time. "So let's make it worth the lie."

Ahead, Tova hears us and barks over her shoulder, "Less chatter, heroes. The forest listens."
But her voice softens on the next breath. "And for the record, Jules—worth doesn't come from dying. It comes from who remembers you."

By nightfall, the outpost rises—steel tower jutting from cracked concrete, drones buzzing in and out of bays. Fence glowing faint blue, electric. Two guards pacing the perimeter.

"This is it," Cassian whispers. "Tova, eyes up for drones. Elia, Jules—you're with me."

The plan sounds simple: breach the fence, plant the disruptor, slip out clean.
Simple, like striking a match. Simple, until it burns.

We crawl close. Cassian cuts a wire, sparks spitting. He slips through first, shadow-quiet. Jules next. Then me.

And that's when one guard turns. His visor flashes moonlight. His gaze lands on me.

"Hey!"

No alarm. No shout for backup. He just charges.

I freeze.

Cassian intercepts, knife flashing, but the guard is bigger. He slams Cassian back. Metal scrapes. The struggle twists—then breaks.

The guard lunges for me.

Instinct kicks. My hand closes on a rock. I swing. Hard.

The crack echoes. The guard drops.

Still. Too still.

Blood spreads black in the dirt. My hands drip red.

"Move!" Cassian barks, dragging me forward. I stumble, half-sick, as he jams the disruptor into the console. Lights stutter. Drones falter, spiraling out of the sky.

But another guard bursts from cover—rifle raised.

Jules doesn't think. He hurls himself forward, slamming the rifle aside. A shot sears wild into the tower wall.

The guard recovers faster. Another shot.

Jules jerks. Falls.

"No!" My scream rips the night. He hits the dirt, blood blooming across his chest.

Tova dives before the echo fades. Her hands press hard, practiced. She's muttering under her breath—numbers, maybe prayers. "Stay with me, kid. Don't you—" She stops mid-word. The life under her palms fades.

"It's no good," she mutters. Flat. Final. "He's gone."

The world empties. The only sound left: the disruptor humming.

Cassian grabs my arm, yanking me from Jules's body.

"We have to move."

I dig my heels in, staring. The boy who smiled at me hours ago. Who believed in proof. His eyes are glass now.

"Now!" Cassian roars, and his voice shoves me into motion.

We sprint. Forest blurs past, drones crashing behind us. My lungs tear with fire. Branches slice skin. My palms are sticky with blood.

When we stop, miles away, the Hollow's shadows swallow us.

I collapse against a tree, gagging, then vomiting until my throat burns raw.

Tova doesn't flinch. She crouches beside me, face grim. "This is war," she says softly. "There's no clean survival. Don't fool yourself."

Her voice has lost its bite. She pulls a flask from her jacket and takes a long swig before handing it to me. "He wasn't ready," she murmurs. "None of them ever are."

I shake my head, throat tight. "You didn't even—"
"Cry?" she finishes for me. "I learned to do that quiet, years ago. Back when they still gave us body bags."

She presses her hand over her medpack, like she's feeling the ghosts inside it. "I've carried more names than I can count. Jules just joined them."

Her words shouldn't comfort me, but somehow they do. There's something in the way she says *names*, not *numbers*.

Cassian stands apart. Watching. Silent. No comfort. No words.

The silence is worse than the blood.

That night, the camp quiets, but my mind doesn't. Every time I blink, I see Jules falling—the look of shock, not pain, the question he never got to ask.

He used to talk about static: how every Dominion broadcast carried ghosts beneath the noise, half-deleted code whispering old truths. He said if you listened long enough, you could hear the world remembering itself.

Maybe that's what I hear now—the world remembering him.

Before dawn, I stumble outside. Fog curls thick. Trees loom skeletal. Above, the Dominion's grid hums faint, static crackling like broken glass.

I stare up, hands trembling though they're clean now. Clean, but not.

There's no going back. Not to the girl who hid her wrist. Not even to the girl who survived the Forge.

Blood rewrites you.

Jules is gone. The guard is gone. And I'm still here. Alive. But not the same.

The static above buzzes louder, prickling against my Mark.
Warning. Or promise.
Maybe both.

Chapter 12

Memories That Burn

The Hollow sleeps.
I don't.

The forest presses too close—shadows stretched long across crooked huts, smoke curling from dying fires like restless ghosts. I sit on the pallet, knees pulled up, Jules's face still burned on the back of my eyelids every time I blink.

When sleep finally drags me under, it doesn't bring rest.
It brings memory.

I'm thirteen again.

The Marking Hall looms—a cathedral of steel and light. Rows of children shoulder to shoulder, wrists bare, fear sharp in the air like ozone. Dominion banners hang red, black, white—their insignia glaring down like an eye that never closes.

Names are called. One by one, a child steps forward, lays their arm on the console. A Mark sears into skin. Green. Amber. Blue. Red.
Some cry. Some faint.

When they call mine—*Dareth, Elia*—my legs nearly fold.

The console is ice under my palm. The needle descends.

And then fire.

Crimson explodes across my wrist, burning like molten glass. I cry tears from my throat. Gasps ripple through the hall as red spreads, alive and searing.

The official's face flickers—satisfaction, then calculation. He stamps the record. "Crimson. Confirmed."

The crowd recoils.

And in the back row—my parents.

Now, in memory, I see them clearer than I did then. My mother pale, clutching my father's arm like she's drowning. My father's jaw tight, eyes wild.
Not grief. Not shock.
Terror.

When the ceremony ends, they rush me out. Neighbors avert their eyes. Whispers follow us home.

Inside, the lights stay off. My mother paces, wringing her hands. My father mutters words I didn't understand then, but do now:
"Altered metrics."
"Pre-flagged."
"Uncontrolled input."

I sit on the floor, clutching my wrist, the Mark throbbing like it's alive. "What does it mean?"

My mother kneels, stroking my hair, crying too hard to answer.
My father slams his fist against the table. "This wasn't supposed to happen."

The memory bends, dream warping into nightmare.

Dawn seeps through curtains. I wake to hushed voices in the kitchen.
My mother's voice, breaking: "If they know—"
My father: "Then we're already dead."

A hum outside.
A Dominion car, black and sleek, rolling to the curb.

Uniformed men at the door.
My mother presses a kiss to my forehead, whispering too fast to catch. My father's hand heavy on my shoulder, trembling.

Then they're dragged into the car.
The door slams.
Silence.

And I am left with Crimson burning on my wrist.

I wake with a gasp. Smoke clings to my throat. The hut is dark, only the ember-glow of dying fires leaking through the cracks. My Mark pulses hot, like it remembers too.

I can't sit with it. Not tonight.

Ansel's hut smells of parchment and herbs, ink and dust. He sits hunched over a table, lamp low, spectacles sliding down his nose.

"You couldn't sleep," he says without looking up.

"Do you ever?" I rasp.

He smiles faintly. "Rarely."

I sink onto the bench opposite. "I dreamed of my Marking."

His eyes sharpen. "And?"

"My parents weren't just afraid," I whisper. "They were terrified. They used words I didn't understand. Metrics. Inputs. Like... they knew something."

Ansel leans back, fingers steepled. "And what do you think they meant?"

The thought coils in me, tight. "That maybe my Mark wasn't just predicted. Maybe it was planted."

The words taste dangerous once they're out.

Ansel studies me for a long moment, and the lamplight catches on the faint burns along his knuckles. When he finally speaks, his voice is quiet but sure.
"The Dominion guards its code like holy text. But

there are whispers. Files sealed. Trials erased. It's possible your parents saw more than they should have."

He pauses, a shadow flickering across his face. "I spent years inside their systems—believing data could save us. Believing order was mercy. I was wrong." He looks down at his hands, the same hands that now shake ever so slightly. "What they did to you... to anyone... that isn't prediction. It's control rewritten as salvation."

My palms press flat to the table. "Then why take them? Why not me?"

"Because you are the anomaly," Ansel says softly. "And anomalies are more useful alive than dead."

My throat closes. Alive—but never free. Alive, but only to be studied.

He exhales slowly, the sound more ache than breath. "What they created can be broken, Elia. You're proof of that. Don't mistake their fear for your purpose."

I stare at my wrist. Crimson glows faint in lamplight, pulsing like a second heart.

I hear my father's voice: *This wasn't supposed to happen.* I see the black car.

And for the first time, the fear I've carried since thirteen doesn't feel like fear.
It feels like fire.

"My fate wasn't predicted," I whisper.

Ansel tilts his head. "No?"

I lift my wrist. Crimson burns faint but steady.

"It was planted."

The words hang between us like sparks over dry grass.

Ansel's gaze holds mine—steady, unflinching. "Then maybe," he says gently, "your fire was never theirs to control."

The silence that follows isn't hollow anymore.
It's waiting.
Alive.
A heartbeat between what was written—and what might still be rewritten.

Chapter 13

The Glitch in the System

The Hollow hums like it's half alive, half machine.
Rebels sharpen blades. Patch rifles. Argue over maps.
Smoke curls with mist. And under it all—another
hum, quieter, steadier.

Not drones. Not the Dominion's.
Our own.

Generators stuffed under tarps. Terminals scavenged
from old outposts. Cables knotted through dirt like
veins.
The Hollow pretends it's wild. But it breathes with
circuitry too.

Today Cassian takes me to the center of it.

The "code tent" looks plain from outside—canvas
patched with scrap, sagging under dew. Inside, it
pulses with life.
Screens glow in corners, wired to car batteries. Holo-
threads hang from the ceiling, strands of green light
like veins pulled from the sky. The air reeks of burnt
coffee, solder, and sleeplessness.

And at the center: **Lennox.**

He looks maybe twenty, but exhaustion makes him
timeless. His hair sticks up in a dozen wrong
directions, a streak of copper wire twisted through it
like an accidental crown. Eyes ringed dark, shirt half-

buttoned, boots untied. His hands blur across a keyboard made from three different Dominion models. A mug of something that might once have been coffee steams beside him, labeled in fading marker: **"DON'T TOUCH—SERIOUSLY."**

When we step in, he doesn't look up. "Cassian, you brought me the glitch?"

My back stiffens. "Excuse me?"

Now he glances over. His grin is sharp, tired—but not cruel. "Relax, Crimson. That's a title here, not an insult."

Cassian's jaw flexes. "Watch it, Lennox."

"Wouldn't dream of it," he mutters, but there's a smirk hiding in his voice. He raises his mug in mock salute. "Come on, anomaly girl. Time to meet your reflection."

He waves me closer, deeper into the light.

The holo-threads hum as I step beneath them— columns of gold and green twisting upward like DNA. Each pulse feels like a heartbeat, mechanical and cold.

"This is the Dominion's god," Lennox says, voice halfway between awe and mockery. "The Predictive Algorithm. Arbiter, they call it. Feed it enough data— blood, breath, the twitch of your eye when you lie—

and it tells you who you are, who you'll be, and when you'll die."

A chill snakes through me. The threads weave like veins—endless, pulsing, alive.

"Science dressed as prophecy," Lennox mutters. "I used to believe in it."

Cassian glances over. "You built for them."

"Until I realized what they were building on top of me." He snorts softly. "The Arbiter didn't predict that part."

He flicks his wrist and a strand brightens—a full record. Birth charts, biometrics, a clean endpoint. Cause of death: cardiovascular failure. Age: 63.

"Green Mark," Lennox says. "Predictable. Algorithm loves boring."

Another strand: amber, fractured. Cause of death: unstable variables. Age: 34.

"Ambers. Messy ones."

Then crimson. A violent pulse, jagged, fierce.
Endpoint stamped hard.
Cause of death: violent. Age: 18.

My chest seizes. "That's me."

"Not exactly," Lennox says. "That's every Crimson but you."

He pulls up another strand.
My name burns at the top: **DARETH, ELIA. CRIMSON. FLAGGED.**
The line sputters downward, jagged and broken.
Biometrics flash erratic, blink out. Neural scans flare red.

And the end—
Nothing.

No endpoint. No neat death stamp. Just static fizzing into blank space.

I stumble back. "What... what does that mean?"

Lennox leans in, eyes bright and fevered—the kind of intensity born from too many nights without sleep and too much hope to kill. "It means you don't end."

He taps the static thread. "The Arbiter runs on certainty. Doesn't need to be right—just believable. People follow it. Obey it. That makes it real. Self-fulfilling code." He gestures toward the blank. "But you? You're the first error I've ever seen that the system couldn't overwrite."

"I don't—" My voice shakes. "I don't understand."

"You're Crimson with no endpoint," Lennox says softly. "The code can't see past you."

Cassian's tone is low. "Unreadable."

Lennox grins faintly. "Unpredictable is one thing. Unreadable? That terrifies them."

My arms fold around myself. "So that's why they fear me."

"That's why *everyone* fears you," Lennox says, voice cooling. "Dominion thinks you're the glitch that'll unravel their god. Rebels think you're a weapon that might misfire."

I swallow hard. "And you? What do you think?"

For once, his sarcasm falters. His grin fades. He stares at the flickering static, jaw tightening.

"I think you're proof," he whispers. "Proof the Arbiter isn't perfect. Proof fate isn't fixed. Proof this empire can bleed."

The tent falls quiet except for the hum of power lines and the faint tremor of rain against canvas.

Cassian stands still, storm locked behind his eyes. Lennox sips his bitter coffee, gaze never leaving the broken thread.

And me—I can't breathe.

All my life, Crimson meant death. Nineteen years, if that. Doomed. A curse written in code.

But now—now it's worse.
Not doomed.
Undefined.

And in a world addicted to certainty, *undefined* is more dangerous than death.

Lennox leans back, rubbing at the scar that disappears into his collar—a thin, pale line shaped like circuitry. "You're not marked to die, Elia."

The static flares brighter, sparks shivering through the air.

"You're marked to break death as they've defined it."

The words hang heavy, impossible to unhear.

And I understand:
The Dominion doesn't just fear me.

It can't *see* me at all.

A long beat passes. The hum deepens.

Cassian's voice breaks the silence. "You shouldn't have shown her this."

Lennox's eyes flicker, the old grin returning—defensive this time. "You brought her here. Don't get righteous now."

"I brought her to see the data," Cassian says. "Not to feed your obsession."

"Obsession?" Lennox laughs, hollow. "You think I'm doing this for fun? I'm trying to dismantle a god, Cassian. You fight it with guns—I fight it with code."

Cassian steps forward, close enough the air feels tight between them. "Just remember which side you're on."

Lennox doesn't blink. "I'll remember when the sides stop shifting."

The two of them hold the stare—a static line between loyalty and distrust—until Cassian finally turns away.

"Come on, Elia," he says, voice clipped. "We're done here."

But as I follow him out, I glance back.

Lennox is still at the console, hands hovering above the light, watching the static pulse like it's alive—like it's whispering to him alone.

For a moment, I wonder which side he's really on. Then the tent flap closes behind me, and the hum fades into rain.

Chapter 14

The Map in Her Blood

You can feel the nervous energy.
Word of the mission—Jules's death, the guard I
killed, the drones we blinded—spreads like smoke.
Some whisper proof the Dominion can bleed. Others
whisper proof I'm too dangerous to keep.
I don't answer either.

When the murmurs grow too loud, Cassian finds me.
"Ansel wants you." That's all he says. But I catch
something under his tone—tension that didn't exist
before the code tent. Lennox's name doesn't leave his
mouth, yet it sits in the silence between us.

Ansel's hut is darker than usual, shutters pulled tight.
Lantern light etches his face in fire and shadow. On
the table: not one scroll this time. Stacks. Ancient
leather, frayed edges, ink curling into strange symbols.

He doesn't greet me. Just gestures. "Sit."
I do, chest already tight.

"These texts," he begins, "predate the Dominion by
centuries. Back when city-states warred. When
Predictive science was new. Marks then were
warnings, not brands."
His fingers skim one scroll—spirals, jagged lines, a
circle of flame. "They spoke of the Bloodmarked.
Veins carrying anomalies the models couldn't cage."

My heart jolts. "Bloodmarked."

Ansel nods. "Most were crushed, erased. But some texts speak of one destined to return when the machine pressed too heavy on its own people. A Crimson Spark."

He unfurls another parchment—symbols of flame, water, shattered glass. At the center, a crude wrist, veins branching like rivers.
"They said the Spark would not carry prophecy written by gods. It would carry a map written in blood. A living thread leading to the system's end."

I shake my head, pulling back. "No. Stop."

"Elia—"

"I'm not a prophecy." My voice cracks sharp. "I'm not your Crimson Spark. Not a blood map. I'm just a girl who can't get someone else's blood off her hands."

Jules's face flashes in my mind—his body in the dirt.

Ansel's eyes soften, though his voice stays firm. "You may not want it. But it may want you."

He lays another manuscript on the table. Newer ink, tighter script, same symbols repeating.
"Copied by one of the first rebels," he explains. "They noticed something. The Bloodmarked's scars weren't inert. They resonated. Marks glowed near nodes—data towers, surveillance grids, control hubs."

I freeze.

The outpost. Jules's death. The console sparking. The burn in my wrist.

Not adrenaline. Something else.

"Like it was syncing," I whisper.

Ansel nods slowly.

He leans forward, voice low like the walls might listen. "What if your DNA isn't accident? What if it traces back to the architects of the algorithm itself? What if you are not outside the mirror, Elia... but the crack in it?"

The words thrum through me like the Mark's pulse.

"No." I back away, shaking my head. "That means I'm not me. That means I'm just... their code, walking around in skin."

Ansel doesn't argue. He lets the silence burn.

Somewhere beyond the hut, I hear the faint buzz of a generator—the same uneven rhythm Lennox coaxed back to life in the code tent. I wonder if he's still awake, staring at the static version of my name, trying to decode what he couldn't explain. A part of me wants to ask him if he knew this was coming—if his glitch found its echo in Ansel's prophecy.

I push back from the table, pacing. "You all talk like I'm a weapon. A prophecy. A glitch made to break things. Do you even hear yourselves? You're turning me into the Dominion's reflection."

My fists clench. "I don't want to be code. I don't want to be prophecy. I want to be Elia."

The words echo too loud in the cramped room.

And then a voice answers from the doorway. "You are."

I whirl. Cassian. Shadows draped across him. His storm-gray eyes steady on me.

"You're not their weapon," he says, stepping inside. "Not ours either. You choose."

A bitter laugh claws up my throat. "Easy for you to say. You're not carrying this."

He closes the space, slow but certain, until his presence presses against mine. "You think I don't know what it's like? To be forged into something I didn't choose?" His voice rough, low. "Every scar on me is a command I never wanted. The only choice left is what to do with them."

His gaze softens—just a fraction. "That's what you have. Choice."

For a long moment, I can't speak. The smoke, the parchments, the whispers of sparks and maps—all pressing down. My skin too tight, my chest too full.

But when I look at my wrist, at the faint glow of Crimson in the lamplight, I don't flinch.

For the first time, I let it burn.
Not curse. Not prophecy.
Part of me.
Part of what I'll choose.

I lift my eyes—first to Ansel, then to Cassian. My
voice steadier than I expect.
"Maybe I am a crack in their mirror. But cracks don't
only break."

The Mark pulses once, heat alive in my blood.
"Sometimes they let the light in."

Cassian's breath catches—just slightly. In that
heartbeat I see it: the war between fear and faith. And
maybe, behind it, a memory of the static screen in
Lennox's tent and the danger it revealed.

Because whatever happens next, none of them—
Cassian, Ansel, or Lennox—can unsee what I am
now.
And somewhere in the Hollow, I know Lennox is
watching the power grids flicker, rewriting lines of
code that could decide which of us survives the dawn.

And I don't look away.

Chapter 15

A Heart Divided

Training never ends in The Hollow. Rebels rise with the sun and spar in the ash clearing until sweat soaks into dirt; drills follow—raids, rescues, the steady rhythms of war. Every strike is practice, every breath a lesson in surviving what comes next.

Cassian trains harder than anyone. He never makes a show of it—no shouting, no flourish—but his movements are precise and merciless, iron shaped until it forgets it was ever soft. Today he's the one teaching me.

The staff in my hands feels heavier than it should. Polished wood, simple, and already blistering my palms. He circles me, storm-gray eyes searching, finding every flaw.

"Your stance," he says. "Too high. You'll topple."

I drop lower, knees bent.

"Better. Again."

Wood cracks against wood. After the third strike my arms complain; after the fifth they burn. He never pulls his blows, and he never breaks me—only pushes, sharpens, makes the edges hold. When I stumble he doesn't catch me. "Up," he orders. When I swing wide he knocks the staff clean from my hands. "Again."

Hours blur. Sweat soaks my shirt and bruises bloom beneath it, but I rise every time because I refuse to let him see me stay down. At last dusk bleeds through the trees and Cassian lowers his staff. "That's enough," he says, and I collapse into the dirt, lungs heaving, everything trembling.

When the camp quiets and the others drift to their huts, I find the small fire Cassian has built at the edge of the clearing. Sparks lift and vanish into the canopy; the Hollow hums soft around us. He sits opposite, no blade this time, rolling a scrap of charcoal between his fingers. The raven tattoo on his neck drinks the light.

"You never get tired, do you?" I ask, voice rough.

His mouth twitches—almost a smile. "Always. I just don't show it."

For the first time he looks less like stone and more like someone who has been made to hold too much. He studies the fire a long moment, then, without looking at me, says, "You asked why I knew your name. Why I knew what you were."

My spine tightens.

"I was raised in their halls," he murmurs. "Not here. Inside the Dominion." The words land like metal.

He tells me of being taken young with his brother, of training and conditioning until loyalty was survival and obedience was strength. Feeling, they said, was weakness. When I picture him as a boy, his storm eyes stripped of softness, my chest aches.

"How did you leave?" I whisper.

"Lucien pulled us out," he says. "But what they forged doesn't disappear. It waits."

Silence presses between us, heavy and sharp. Then he lifts his gaze.

"There's something else you need to know."

My pulse jumps. "What?"

"That night in New Virelia," he says. "When you thought the Dominion had slipped into your flat—the scrape of boots, drawers opening."

My world tilts. "It was you?"

He does not flinch. "I was sent to confirm. Before we risked this camp on you, I had to see with my own eyes if the files were right—Crimson, seventeen, alive, not already broken."

My stomach twists. "So you prowled through my life while I slept, like I was... prey."

"Yes." His voice is rough but steady. "I watched. I left when I saw you still fighting, even in sleep. I slipped a coded speaker into the wall before I left to test you—see whether panic or endurance lived in you when the air itself turned against you. You didn't break. That's when I knew you were stronger than their files claimed."

Anger flares hot and bitter. "And in the square? You were supposed to let them end me."

His storm-gray eyes meet mine without flinching. "That was the plan. I should have stood by. I didn't. I stepped in because I couldn't watch them erase you." He hesitates, then adds in a quieter voice, "I knew bringing you here was right, even if Lucien and others didn't fully agree."

The fire spits and sends sparks scattering. "And now?" I ask. "What are you supposed to do with me here?"

He crushes the charcoal between his fingers until ash smears his skin. "If you fracture—if you lose yourself—it will put the Hollow in danger. My role is simple: protect the rebels. If that means ending you first, then I have to carry that weight."

The words hollow me out. "So even now… you're still the blade at my throat."

"No." His voice sharpens, steadier. "I keep the Hollow breathing. That means watching you closer than anyone else. It doesn't mean I want the blade to fall."

I look away, chest tight, and something older surfaces: the first time my implant blinked in the square and found him blank where a name and color should have been.

"My implant," I say. "It tried to read you and found nothing. Everyone registers—everyone but you."

He is quiet a long time. Then he pushes back his sleeve to show me a pale scar, a thin line carved across the vein where registry once was. "To the Dominion, I don't exist," he says. "Lucien scrubbed my registry when we left the halls. No number. No category. No expiration date."

"Blank," I echo.

He nods. "Your implant glitched because it reached for me and found nothing. I'm the error their system can't fix. An anomaly."

"That's... impossible," I murmur.

"A lot of what survived us looks impossible," he replies with a bitter, small smile. "But here I am."

The firelight throws shadows across his face. Slowly, without deciding, I reach and let my hand brush his. He goes rigid for a heartbeat, storm-gray eyes locking on mine, but he does not withdraw.

"The more I care," he says, voice raw, "the worse this ends."

He doesn't look away. "But I care anyway."

His confession hangs between us—fragile and dangerous as glass. I know, in the hollow of that moment, that whatever this is will break us both. Still, I cannot let go.

Chapter 16

Lucien's Doubt

After each mission the air shifts—tighter, sharper. Rebels haul water, sharpen blades, argue over maps, but their eyes keep flicking to the tree line. Voices drop when a drone hums on the horizon. This time the tension cuts deeper.

I feel it in the stares that follow me, in whispers that curl like smoke. She's the anomaly, they say. The Dominion senses her. She'll bring them here. Maybe they're right. When my Mark flares, I swear the sky answers back, louder, like it's listening.

Cassian slips away before dawn. I watch him follow Lucien into the war room—a squat hut armored with steel plates nailed over rotten wood—and then the door slams. Commanders only. The rest of us are left to guess. Guesses don't hold when the stakes are this high. So I wait.

A courier slips out with a stack of maps and I catch the door before it shuts, moving quiet and careful. Inside, lantern light pools over a table gouged by knives and stained with ink. Lucien stands at the head, his voice colder than the metal bolting the walls. On the table, in the center, my name is written on a map.

"Our scouts intercepted transmissions last night," Lucien announces, slamming his palm on the parchment. "Dominion sensors pinged irregularities by the northern grid. They're triangulating. And we know what's drawing them."

Silence spreads. Cassian's voice cuts in, low and steady. "There's no proof it's her."

Lucien's glare snaps. "There's no proof it isn't. We've seen her Mark near nodes. It hums like a beacon. She is the beacon."

Mira leans forward, wiry and hard-eyed. "If she's drawing sensors, she's compromised us. We can't risk the Hollow for one Crimson."

Lucien doesn't rise to anger; his calm is colder, surgical. "Then we don't risk it. We use it." He spreads maps across the table—valleys, choke points, ridges inked in red. "Let her draw their forces into the burned valley. Collapse the ridge. One trap, hundreds dead, their outpost crippled."

The room reacts—shock, protest, reluctant nods. "She's one girl," Lucien presses. "Her sacrifice buys us a year."

A commander recoils. "We're not executioners. If we use our own as bait, we become them."

Arguments collide like flint—fear sparking against principle. Someone calls her too dangerous to shelter. Someone else says she's proof the system can break. Someone says she's already a liability; someone, that she could be the key. Under it all, Lucien's refrain cuts like a blade: "Sacrifice one to save thousands. That's war."

Cassian stands silent, fists clenched. At last he says, "If you do this, you'll lose more than you gain. You'll lose the Hollow's soul."

Lucien's eyes flash. "This isn't about soul. It's about survival."

The silence that follows is heavier than any sword. I do not stay to hear more. The words have already burned in. Use her. Sacrifice one. Save thousands.

I stumble into the cold with my lungs tight and my heartbeat a jagged thing. Faces turn as I pass—curiosity, wariness, suspicion. The rebellion was supposed to mean choice, freedom. Lucien's voice now sounds no different from the Dominion's—measuring lives, counting bodies. My father's old words echo in my head: This wasn't supposed to happen. Maybe it always was.

I don't go back to the hut. I don't look for Cassian or Ansel or anyone. I run until the trees swallow me. My Mark burns hot, a flare impossible to hide. They want prophecy, they want a Crimson spark, a bloodmarked map—a symbol to bargain with or to break. Fine. But I will not be their pawn. Not Dominion. Not rebels.

The fire in my blood thrums louder, alive and dangerous. "They want prophecy?" I whisper into the dark; my voice shakes. The Mark sears hotter under my skin. "Then I will give them a reckoning."

Chapter 17

The Breaker Tower Raid

The Hollow never truly sleeps when war is near.
Word spreads like sparks on dry leaves: the
Dominion's Breaker Tower—one of their main relay
hubs—is streaming its nightly feed. Gleaming
soldiers. Obedience speeches. Endless loops of
Crimson executions.

Not just surveillance. Control.

Taking it down would hurt them.

So blades are sharpened. Charges packed. Quiet
prayers whispered.

Cassian finds me before dawn. His voice is flat,
unreadable.
"Lucien wants a team for the Breaker Tower. You're
in it."

I should refuse. I should tell him I'm done being their
pawn, their proof, their risk. But the hum under my
skin won't let me. Every time I see Dominion steel,
something in me answers it. Defiance. Fire.
So I nod. "Fine."

For a moment, his jaw tenses—like he's about to say
something else. But he just nods, once.
When he turns away, I catch it—a tremor in his
breath, gone too quickly to be weakness.

We meet in the training pit—half dirt, half metal. Tova's already there, cleaning her sidearm with one hand while chewing on a strip of dried root. "Ah, the prodigal anomaly arrives," she says without looking up.

Next to her, a figure crouches in the dust, tracing a map of the Breaker compound with a stick.

Ren.

He's hard to place at first glance—lean and wiry, maybe my age, his hair dark and ragged like it's been hacked off with a blade. A scar runs through his left brow, shallow but old. His voice, when he finally speaks, is barely more than a whisper.

"Four guards per tower level. Two on each catwalk. They rotate every seven minutes."

His finger moves over the dirt map—precise, practiced.

Cassian nods. "You've scouted it?"

Ren glances up, eyes pale and sharp as frost. "Three times. Closest I've been without losing a drone." His gaze flicks to me then, assessing. Not hostile—just measuring, like he's cataloguing exits and weaknesses all at once.

"Ren used to track defectors through the marsh lines," Tova explains. "Before he decided the wrong side was paying his rations."

Ren doesn't confirm or deny it. "Tracking's tracking," he murmurs. "Now I follow ghosts that wear armor."

He folds the map shut with a sweep of his boot, then meets my eyes. "You don't need to keep up," he says quietly. "Just stay in step."
Something about it isn't arrogance—it's warning.

The team:
Cassian—sharp and storm-eyed as ever.
Tova—the medic whose sarcasm cuts deeper than her scalpel.
Ren—the silent scout who sees every shadow before it moves.
And me.

The plan: slip through the old service tunnels, plant Lennox's virus in the relay core, and set charges to bring the tower down—cutting the Dominion's streams across half the region.

"High risk, high reward," Tova mutters while checking her gear. "Lucien's favorite kind of suicide."

Cassian says nothing. His hands move steadily, loading a rifle with mechanical calm—but his knuckles are white on the grip. When our eyes meet for the briefest second, I see something in his expression that doesn't belong there: regret.

Tova glances up from her medpack. "You ever notice the men in charge never carry stretchers? Just orders."

When Cassian doesn't respond, she smirks faintly and shoves a syringe into her pocket. "Don't worry, Commander. I'll stitch you up after you nearly get us killed."

Her humor lands brittle. I catch her rubbing the scar on her thigh—an old burn twisting down toward her knee. Later, when the others move off, she catches me looking.

"Dominion plasma mine," she says. "Year one of the rebellion. I walked it off."

"Walked?"

She shrugs. "Crawled first. Cursed a lot. Then walked."

It's not pride. It's proof of endurance.

Lennox presses a small spike into my palm. "You're the glitch. Their scanners can't read you right. You'll get closest." His grin fades when he sees my expression. "Don't get caught, Crimson. Or we're all ash."

I squeeze the spike until my knuckles ache.

Cassian lingers at the edge of the clearing as we prepare to move. His eyes trace every buckle on my gear, every strap, like he's searching for excuses to delay the mission. Finally, his hand brushes my shoulder—barely a touch, just enough for the words that follow to feel heavier.

"Stay behind me in the tunnels," he says. "No heroics."

I raise a brow. "I thought that was your specialty."

Something flickers across his mouth—a ghost of a smile. It doesn't reach his eyes.

The tower rises above the forest like a wound—steel ribs twisting toward the sky, screens bleeding propaganda across the dark. Drones circle in thick clouds, their blue beams cutting through the mist.

We crawl through damp tunnels slick with rot, water dripping from fractured pipes. Every step echoes too loud. Cassian leads, silent and precise, the rhythm of a soldier who's lived too many missions.

Ren scouts ahead, his movements soundless. He moves like the forest itself—vanishing, reappearing, hand signals crisp and economical. Even in the dark, his focus cuts clean through the chaos.

"Drone sweep in ten seconds," he murmurs once, voice low enough to vanish beneath the drip of water. We freeze, holding breath until the hum fades. Then he gestures—two fingers forward—and we move.

Tova limps slightly but never slows. She moves like someone who's decided pain is just another language. When Ren signals another drone ahead, she tosses a small flare pellet, drawing its beam away. "See?" she whispers. "Still good for something besides stitching holes."

Cassian glances back at her, then at me, his jaw tightening as if he wants to speak—then doesn't. Every unspoken word builds like pressure under his skin.

The relay chamber hums like a living heart—wires coiled and glowing, Dominion code flowing in

pulsing light. The air buzzes with energy.
"Now," Cassian says.

My Mark burns hot against my wrist. I step forward
as scanners sweep across us—then glitch, flooding
with static instead of alarms. They can't read me.
I drive the spike into the core.

The tower convulses. Screens warp. Dominion voices
splinter into white noise. For a breath, victory tastes
real—sharp and electric.

Then the alarms explode.

Drones dive, beams slicing the air. Soldiers pour
through the doors. Tova's already firing, her precision
terrifying. "You'd think after all these years they'd run
out of bullets," she growls, reloading.

Ren fires back, quick and deliberate. One of the
Dominion soldiers flanks right; Ren drops him with a
single, clean shot. Another grazes him; blood splashes
his sleeve. Tova curses, shoving a tourniquet on him
even as she shoots over his shoulder. "Stay still or I
swear I'll tranquilize you myself!"

Cassian moves like a storm—blade flashing, gunfire
cutting clean through the chaos. But there's
something off in his rhythm tonight. Hesitation. He
keeps glancing toward me, between shots, like every
move risks breaking an invisible order.

"Charges!" he shouts.

Ren scrambles, planting explosives along the struts while sparks rain from the ceiling. The tower groans beneath its own weight.
"Thirty seconds!"

We run.

Tova stumbles; a drone grazes her side. Smoke blooms crimson where the beam touched skin. Cassian catches her under one arm, dragging her forward. "I'm fine," she gasps. "Don't you dare waste effort."

The escape tunnel yawns ahead. Cassian drags Tova through first, Ren clutching the trigger. I'm only steps behind when the steel barrier slams down.

A hiss of hydraulics. The door seals.

I crash into it, pounding my fists. "Cassian!"

Through the narrow slit of glass, I see him—storm-gray eyes. Steady. Silent.
But not cold.
There's pain there—sharp, deliberate, held behind restraint. His lips move, almost soundless. *I'm sorry.*

He doesn't open the door. Doesn't let himself.
Then he turns. Pulls the others with him.
Leaves me.

The tower trembles, explosions tearing through its spine. Smoke floods the chamber. Drones swarm in from above, beams slicing through what's left.

Panic claws at my throat. I stumble through the haze, coughing, searching for a way out. My hands find a side hatch, rusted shut. I tear at it until my palms bleed.

The Mark flares white-hot, fire surging through my veins. With a scream, I wrench the hatch free and crawl through as the tower collapses behind me.

Metal rakes my skin raw. I spill into the forest, choking on smoke, body torn and shaking. Behind me, the tower folds inward on itself, a shrieking monument of fire and steel.

And I am alone.

The smoke blurs into memory. Thirteen again—the Marking Hall, my parents' pale faces, their whispers sharp and frightened. The Dominion car waiting outside. The door slamming. The silence that followed.

Betrayal. Abandonment.

Now it overlays the present—another steel door, another pair of eyes turning away. The same silence.

I limp through the ash-choked trees, not knowing if I'm heading toward the Hollow or just deeper into nothing. Blood streaks the moss; my chest burns with every breath.

Somewhere behind the ringing in my ears, I hear Tova's voice from before the raid—half-mocking, half-kind: "Worth doesn't come from dying. It comes from who remembers you."

She's probably bleeding out in a tunnel she refused to call fatal. But she'll still be thinking of everyone else first.

I trusted the rebellion. Trusted Cassian.
They left me.
Just like the Dominion. Just like my parents.

The Mark burns hotter—not as curse or omen, but as fire.
"I trusted the wrong side," I whisper, voice breaking.
"Maybe there isn't a right one."

The words disappear into the smoke, small and bitter.
The forest gives no answer.
Only the steady thrum of the Mark beneath my skin—defiant even now.

Chapter 18

Ash Between Us

The forest doesn't breathe right after the explosion.
It coughs.
It chokes.

Smoke clings low to the ground, wrapping around the roots like ghosts too heavy to rise. I can still hear the echo of the Breaker Tower's collapse—the sound of Dominion steel folding in on itself, the roar of victory twisted with ruin.

It should feel like triumph.
Instead, it feels like grief.

I stumble through ash and heat, my throat raw, lungs scraping against the smoke. Every movement feels like tearing open a wound. My body is alive, but only just. The rest of me—whatever's left—feels like it's still inside that collapsing tower, screaming.

And under the ringing in my ears, there's one sound I can't silence.
The slam of that steel door.

"Cassian!"

His name still burns the back of my throat.

The memory replays whether I want it to or not: the narrow slit of glass, the storm-gray eyes on the other side, steady and silent. The way he didn't move. Didn't open it. Didn't even *try*.
Just that flash—guilt, maybe. Regret. And then nothing.

He turned.
And left.

For a long time, I told myself I wouldn't be the girl who breaks over someone's silence. But this—this feels worse than any Dominion wound. Because it wasn't the Dominion this time. It was him.

I collapse beside a charred log, coughing until my ribs ache. My hands shake so hard I can't tell where the blood ends and the dirt begins. I press my palms to the earth, grounding myself in something that doesn't lie.

He said once, *Weapons don't choose what they destroy, but they can choose where they aim.*
And I believed him.
I *trusted* him.

I laugh—a cracked, hollow sound. "Guess I aimed wrong."

The forest doesn't answer. Just a slow hiss as burning debris falls in the distance.

For a moment, I think I see movement between the trees—a flicker of shadow, a shape that could be him. My heart lurches. But when I blink, it's gone.

Maybe that's fitting. Cassian was always more shadow than man. You could see him, but never touch what he really was.

I drag myself toward a shallow stream that winds through the ravine, its water gray with ash. I dip my hands in, the cold biting through grime and blood. The reflection staring back at me barely looks human—soot-streaked, eyes hollow, the faint red pulse of my Mark glowing like a wound that won't heal.

"Why did you do it?" I whisper to no one. "Why lock me out?"

My voice shakes, and I hate it. I hate that I care enough to ask.

I slam my fist into the water, sending ripples across the reflection. "You said you chose me." My words come sharper now, rising like the smoke still clawing the sky. "You said you defied orders for me."

A bitter laugh claws its way out. "Guess that ended at the first command that mattered."

I press my forehead to my knees, breath ragged. Every thought tangles with memory—the way he looked at me before the mission, the hesitation he didn't explain, the way his hand brushed mine in the tunnels as if he couldn't help it. All of it feels like a lie now.

And yet—some part of me can't forget what I saw through that glass.
Not indifference. Not cruelty.
Something else.

He looked like a man choosing which part of himself to kill.

"Don't you dare think this saves me," I whisper to the trees, to him, to the world. "You don't get to decide that."

The Mark flares faintly at my wrist, heat threading up my arm. It's not pain this time—it's anger given shape.

For hours, I wander aimlessly through the ruins of the forest. Every sound feels like an echo of what I lost. When I finally collapse against a blackened stump, the exhaustion catches up. My body trembles, skin burning where shrapnel grazed it.

I let myself cry then—not quietly, not cleanly. The kind of cry that leaves your lungs raw and your heart hollow.

I thought I was past this. Past believing anyone could stay.

But Cassian wasn't supposed to be anyone.
He was supposed to be the exception.

The one who saw something more than a curse when he looked at me. The one who told me *I wasn't theirs.*

I should've known better.
The Hollow, the rebellion, the Dominion—they all speak the same language in the end. Sacrifice dressed as strategy.

"Don't get attached," Lucien had told him.
And he listened.

When the tears finally stop, what's left isn't grief. It's resolve.

If Cassian thinks leaving me alive is mercy, he's wrong. Mercy doesn't burn like this.

I push myself up, legs shaking, and turn toward the smoldering remains of the tower. Smoke still rises in thick plumes, black against the dim horizon.

"Fine," I whisper to the ruin. "You want me to survive? I will. But not for you."

The Mark glows brighter, pulsing in rhythm with my heartbeat. A rhythm that refuses to die.

I take one step, then another, until the wind shifts and the ash starts to settle. Somewhere behind it, the Hollow waits. Maybe Cassian does too.

But when I find him, I won't ask *why.*
I'll make him answer.

Because if he thought locking that door would keep me safe—
he doesn't know me at all.

Chapter 19

The Oracle of Ash

The ash forest feels endless.

I pick my way through the skeleton trees, every step a jab—leg throbbing where rust tore it open, arms scraped raw, lungs filled with smoke that refuses to leave. Night and day smell the same here: iron and burned wood. My vision swims, yet I keep moving. Something deeper than survival pulls me forward.

The Mark on my wrist has steadied. No longer the stuttering flare it was after the tower, it pulses softly, like a heartbeat sending code through my veins. I don't know if it guides me or if I'm following the echo inside myself. Either way, I go toward the light.

Through the blackened branches, a faint glow breathes. It isn't Dominion light—softer, red as ember, alive like something that remembers warmth. I follow it down where the ground caves in, where vines strangle the mouth of a cavern. Warm air exhales from the dark, scented with herbs, smoke, and something sharp, like incense and old paper. Symbols are carved above the entrance—circles around a flame, lines branching like rivers.

The hollow opens into a cavern that smells like memory. Torches burn low, red flames that don't lick so much as rest. Ash carpets the floor; the air is dense and muffled beneath my steps. At the center, a dead tree stands hollowed into a shrine, its bark scarred with ember lines that glow faintly like veins.

Figures move through the chamber, cloaked in gray, faces hidden. Their murmurs form a rhythm—half language, half prayer. When they see me, the sound shifts. Not fear. Recognition.

"She has come."
"The Crimson."

From the far side steps a woman whose white hair falls in a braid like a trail of ash. Her eyes are clouded—blind—but her face is mapped with soot symbols. She leans on a staff older than any I've seen. The room calls her by name.
Saria. The Oracle.

She tilts her head toward me, sensing the space. "You walked far, Crimson."

"I didn't know where I was going," I say, my voice thin from smoke.

"You were led," she answers simply. "By your blood. By your Mark."

They call themselves the Remnants—keepers of the books and songs the Dominion tried to burn away. Guardians of things older than the cities above. They gather in a quiet ring around me, not pressing, simply present. Together they speak a creed in one breath: "The Mark was never meant for fear. It was a key. A choice."

The word strikes something inside me—choice— falling deep, rippling outward like a stone dropped into still water. Not curse. Not sentence. Choice.

"Then why does everyone treat it like death?" I ask, because the question has gnawed at me for years.

Saria's head tilts slightly. "Because rulers prefer death. Death obeys. Choice does not." Her blind eyes lift toward me, finding me with a precision that feels impossible. "They turned a lantern into a lock."

She leads me to the hollowed tree and presses her palm against its scorched bark. The ember lines flare faintly at her touch. "The prophecy—if you call it that—is older than the Dominion's code, older than their chains. It speaks of a Crimson who rises when the system strains itself to breaking. Not to die, but to decide."

My throat tightens. "Decide what?"

"Rebellion, or ruin." Two words, blunt and heavy. Both possible.

They unroll scrolls so thin they tremble in the air, their surfaces inked with diagrams and delicate script. Early Marks are sketched in them—soft, exploratory, almost gentle. Warnings once meant to guide, not condemn. But fear crept in, twisting guidance into verdict. Lanterns became cages.

"So Crimson wasn't supposed to mean death?" I ask. The thought tastes like ash and relief.

Saria shakes her head. "It meant potential."

She steps closer, holding a small bowl of ash mixed with oil. The scent is warm, metallic, clean. Dipping her fingers into it, she draws a spiral on my cheek. The touch burns faintly but doesn't hurt. It feels like recognition. "This is not marking," she says softly. "It is opening."

A part of me wants to pull away—another mark, another prophecy, another hand trying to define me. But a quieter voice inside whispers: *This time it's yours.*

I breathe, then nod.

Saria's fingers trail down to my wrist, connecting the spiral to the Crimson. The glow flares brighter, steady and warm like a hearth. The Remnants hum around us. "The choice begins," they murmur.

When she steps back, she draws a dagger from within the hollow tree—a simple blade, edges honed by someone who remembers how to shape steel by hand. Spirals are etched along the metal like veins, mirroring the patterns that run through the tree's scar. She lays it across my palms.

"This is not for blood," she tells me. Her voice is low, unshakable. "It severs fear."

I close my fingers around the hilt and feel its weight settle, balanced and sure. It isn't a weapon. It's a promise. My Mark glows beneath my skin, bright and calm. For the first time, the heat feels wholly mine— not a label, not a sentence. Mine.

The Remnants return to their murmured prayers, words threading through the air like strands of smoke. Saria lowers herself beside the hollow tree, her blind eyes turned upward as if reading the shape of the unseen sky.

I stand in the quiet, ash dusting my cheek, the dagger warm in my grip, the Mark burning with steady light. Choice hums through my bones. Not curse. Not verdict. Choice.

The path ahead is wide and jagged, two ways pulling at the same thread. But this time, I feel the split and know it belongs to me.

I tighten my fingers around the dagger. For the first time since I was thirteen, I shape an answer that is entirely my own.

Chapter 20

Flare of Choice

The Grove Below hums like a quiet heartbeat. Ash and ember light ripple across the cavern walls, painting everything in shades of red and black. The Remnants kneel near the hollow tree, their murmurs blending with the low crackle of fire. They don't worship gods—they keep memory alive. Memory older than the Dominion, older than fear itself.

I sit among them with the dagger resting across my knees. The ash marks on my skin still burn faintly where Saria traced her spiral. For the first time in years, I leave my wrist uncovered. The Crimson shines steady, pulsing against the firelight—not hidden, not denied.

There is no ceremony, no thunderous voice, no vow carved into air. Only firelight, silence, and choice.

A woman kneels before me, setting a shallow basin on the ground. Steam curls from the water, fragrant with herbs that smell sharp and clean. She dips her hands into it and tips the water over mine. Ash and blood slide away, swirling dark into the basin. "You've walked through fire," she murmurs. "Now you decide what remains."

The water cools quickly. Droplets trace the length of my wrist and glisten over the Mark. For years, I buried it beneath sleeves and fabric, desperate to keep eyes from it. Tonight, I lift it high toward the flames.

The fire catches the glow, reflecting it back, and I do not lower it.

When the cleansing ends, they bring me new clothes: robes of black, stitched with faint red thread from root dye. The fabric is soft and light—made not for war but for walking unseen. I pull them over my skin, and they cling like shadow but hold warmth all the same.

Saria's voice fills the chamber, low and certain. "Black for the lost you carry. Red for the fire you keep alive."

The words settle deep. I knot the sash firmly at my waist. For the first time, the Mark on my wrist feels less like a wound carved into me and more like something claimed.

At the center of the cavern, a flat stone glows with heat from buried coals. A shard of steel rests on it, thin and sharpened. Saria's hand finds my shoulder and guides me closer.
"The Crimson belongs to them," she says. "What you carve belongs to you. Mark yourself in what they cannot own."

The steel trembles in my grasp. I press it to the skin just above my wrist. The edge bites—sharp but shallow—enough to draw a flare of blood. I carve a burst, lines radiating outward like sparks breaking free. Blood beads, runs down, and falls into the fire. The flames hiss as if drinking it in.

The glow on my wrist answers, Crimson flaring brighter as the new symbol weaves into it—mine, not theirs.

Through the burn of heat in my throat, I whisper, steady and sure:
"I was not marked to die. I was marked to decide."

The cavern stills.

From the back of the gathering, a small child steps forward, their wrist faint with an amber glow. Dipping a finger into soot, they trace a flare over it, copying mine. Another follows—green streaked with red, amber dusted with coal. Soon, the cavern flickers with dozens of flare symbols painted across glowing wrists.

Saria tilts her head, blind eyes turned upward. "Symbols spread faster than fear."

Hope opens inside me like a second fire, fierce and alive.

I sit with the embers long after, dagger balanced in my lap, the flare burning bright across my wrist. For years, I thought survival was enough. But hiding cost me everything—my parents, Dax, Jules. It stripped away my voice until I barely recognized it.

Now I understand what the Dominion fears most. Not rebellion. Not fire. Not blood. Choice.

The Crimson was never a curse. It was always a key. And I will use it.

When dawn bleeds into the cavern, I rise. My wounds ache, but the fire inside burns hotter than the pain. The Remnants gather quietly to watch as I fasten the dagger at my side and step toward the mouth of the cave.

Saria stands by the hollow tree, her staff rooted in ash. "Go, Crimson Spark. Not as their pawn. Not as their curse. As choice." Her voice is soft, sharp as smoke. "And remember—the blade is not for blood. It is for severing fear."

I bow my head, then climb back into the ash forest.

The ruins of the fallen relay tower rise ahead, steel ribs still smoldering. Smoke drifts upward like black veins against the sky. I walk toward it—not limping now, not bent by fear. My wrist glows high, the flare blazing across my skin.

I am not afraid of the Dominion. Not of Lucien. Not even of Cassian.

Because this time, the story is mine.

I lift my wrist to the dawn, voice steady and unflinching.
"If they see prophecy in me," I whisper, "then it will be one I choose."

Chapter 21

Smoke and Steel

The Hollow doesn't feel the same when I return. Maybe it hasn't changed at all—maybe I have. The forest seems thinner now, the embers colder, every glance sharper than before. Rebels pause at their work as I pass; some tighten their grips on blades, others reach for rifles.

They don't see a girl stumbling back from the ash woods. They see something else—smoke, steel, a shape cut from fire.

I don't bother hiding my wrist anymore. The Crimson burns openly, the flare I carved branching across it, glowing faintly in the firelight like a wound reborn as flame.

Lucien is the first to step forward. The crowd parts instinctively, as if pulled by gravity. His presence presses down on the clearing—part magnet, part blade, charisma sheathed in ruthlessness. He doesn't need to raise his voice to command attention.

At a flick of his hand, weapons lift toward me. "Drop the knife," he says, his tone all iron and order.

I draw the dagger—not to discard it, but to show it. Balanced across my palms, it catches the light. "This isn't for blood," I tell them. "It's for severing fear."

The words ripple through the crowd like wind through tall grass. Some grips soften; others tighten. Lucien's jaw clenches.

"You abandoned us," he says. "You endangered everything. And now you walk back as if this camp still belongs to you?"

I meet his gaze without flinching. "I don't want to own it." I raise my wrist, the crimson blaze steady. "I want to change it."

His eyes narrow. "Cassian's unit returned without you. We assumed you were dead—or worse. Do you understand the risk you put us in?"

I take a step closer. "Do *you*?"

His mouth hardens, but his eyes flicker—too quick for most to see. Guilt, or memory. "You were out of contact. You compromised the mission," he says, each word measured.

The way he says it tells me everything. He knew. He *ordered* it.

"Yes," I answer quietly, though my pulse hammers. "I nearly died. But the danger wasn't in my disappearance. The danger was in your refusal to trust me—or to admit what you did."

A murmur stirs through the rebels, like dry leaves before a storm. Lucien's gaze sharpens, a warning hidden beneath command.

"Watch your tone," he says. "At best, you're a guest here. At worst, a liability."

I shake my head. "No. I'm proof. Proof you've been too afraid to see."

The crowd parts again as Tova limps forward, sarcasm stripped from her face. "She's right," she says flatly. "You saw it, Lucien. Crimson at thirteen. Death before nineteen. Violent. No chance." Her gesture cuts toward me. "And yet—she's still breathing."

Lennox drifts from the shadows, mug in hand, eyes wild from too many sleepless nights. He points toward my wrist where the flare glows against the Crimson.

"The system doesn't glitch," he says. "It bends the world until its prediction comes true. Except with her." He tips the mug toward Lucien. "She broke it. That means the Dominion's god is a fraud."

The words land like sparks on dry tinder.

Lucien's expression doesn't falter, but I see it—the smallest crack in his control, a flash of something buried. Maybe fear. Maybe the weight of what he ordered Cassian to do.

Before he can speak, I step forward. "You fight their towers with bullets," I say, "and every time, the Dominion rebuilds stronger chains. What if, instead of breaking their machines, we used them?"

Lucien's tone cools. "Explain."

I see the image clearly in my mind—the tower collapsing into flame. "A broadcast," I say. "On every screen, every relay. Not their doctrine. Not their silence. Truth. Show the people that the Marks weren't fate—they were control. Show them the algorithm failed."

The air shifts, heavy enough to tilt the ground.

Tova lets out a low whistle. "Broadcast rebellion across the Dominion."

Lennox grins, reckless and bright. "I can lace a virus through their network—thread it like fire through tinder. Spread faster than any soldier can stop it."

Lucien's fury flickers, replaced by something colder. "You'd expose us? Burn every safehouse and shadow we've built?"

"Or," I counter, keeping my voice steady, "we finally let the people see that the Dominion's power only lives in their belief. Break the belief, and you break the chains."

Lucien studies me, the predator in him calculating. "And when the world burns, who decides the cost?"

"I do." My words come out like tempered iron. "Because I wasn't marked to die. I was marked to decide."

The sound that follows feels like wind catching flame—a collective gasp moving through the camp.

Lucien raises a hand for silence, but the rebels aren't looking at him anymore. Their eyes are on me.

Tova leans closer, her voice rough but sure. "I don't trust you, Crimson. But I trust lies even less. If you can break one, I'll stand with you."

Lennox lifts his mug in salute. "Build a signal, burn a god? I'll drink to that."

The tide begins to turn—not completely, but enough.

From the back of the crowd, I feel a weight heavier than rifles or whispers. Cassian. Hood shadowing his face, arms crossed, storm-gray eyes locked on me. He hasn't spoken. He hasn't moved. But he's watching. Always watching.

I don't look back. Not yet.

Lucien's voice cuts through the murmurs, smooth as steel. "You want to lead us into fire? Then prepare to burn beside us."

But the eyes in the clearing are no longer fixed on him. They're fixed on me.

I straighten, the flare blazing across my skin, the dagger steady at my side. Smoke curls through the pits. Steel glints in the shadows. And in that moment, I understand: this is no longer only his rebellion.

Chapter 22

Cassian's Truth

The Hollow never truly sleeps.
Fires gutter low while guards shift their rifles, and
whispers move from hut to hut like restless ghosts.

I slip through the camp without slowing, the cold air
biting deeper as I climb the ridge above. My body
aches—scars tugging, muscles raw—but pain isn't the
loudest thing in me. Louder still are the memories: the
Breaker Tower, the hiss of hydraulics, the moment
Cassian's eyes met mine before he turned away.

I've carried that silence too long.

At the ridge's crest, the old Dominion observatory
waits—its half-dome torn open to the night, ribs of
rust clawing toward the stars. Vines have claimed the
walls, glass shards glint faintly in the moonlight. The
air smells of ash and moss. Still. Tense.

Which is how I know he's here.

Cassian stands in the center, hood pushed back, the
raven ink on his neck catching silver light. His posture
is rigid, soldier-straight—but his stillness feels less like
control tonight, more like bracing for impact.

I don't ease into it. My voice cuts the quiet.
"Why did you leave me?"

He doesn't move, doesn't answer. Just stares at the broken dome as if the sky might hand him a script. When he finally speaks, it's low.
"I knew you'd come."

"That's not an answer."

He exhales, the sound rough and tired. Then turns, and those storm-gray eyes meet mine.
"Because Lucien ordered it."

The words hit like a blade I'd already seen coming—but still bleed anyway.

He steps forward, slow and careful, like every word costs him something.
"If the tower fell, command was to pull back and seal the exit. Tova was hit. We couldn't lose her—the rebellion depends on her for field med and supplies. Lucien said containment was priority. I was supposed to follow protocol."

I laugh once, dry. "And I was what, a liability? Collateral damage?"

His eyes flash—not anger. Pain. "No. You were the exception."

That stops me. "Then why did you obey him?"

Cassian looks away, jaw tightening. "Because I thought... I thought if I disobeyed, he'd send someone else to finish the job. Someone who wouldn't hesitate. Someone who wouldn't care whether you made it out alive."

The words crack something open in him.

He takes another step forward. "Lucien doesn't protect people, Elia. He tests them until they break. If I'd questioned him on the field, he would've seen that you mattered to me—and used it. He would've made sure you didn't walk out of that tower, one way or another."

I blink, stunned by the quiet ferocity in his tone. "You think obeying him *protected* me?"

He nods, slow. "It kept you off his radar. For now."

The bitterness in my chest twists tighter. "So you hurt me to keep me safe."

His shoulders rise, fall. "If it meant you lived—yes."

The silence between us sharpens. My pulse thunders in my ears.

"You watched me through that door," I whisper. "You didn't even try."

"I did," he says softly. "Just not how you think."

I stare, uncertain if I want to believe him.

"I stayed behind after the blast," he continues, voice roughening. "Tracked you through the smoke. I saw

147

you drag yourself into the side tunnel. I covered your escape from the ridge." His gaze drops. "I didn't stop watching until you were out of range."

My throat tightens. "Why?"

He hesitates. Then: "Because I couldn't walk away again."

The admission hangs between us like smoke. He looks older under the moonlight, haunted.

"I don't expect you to forgive me," he says quietly. "Lucien gave the order, but it was still my hand that sealed that door. And that's something I'll carry long after the rebellion burns out."

I sink onto a cracked wall, exhaustion pressing deep into bone. The anger that fueled me up the ridge falters, replaced by something rawer—understanding, maybe, though I don't want to call it that.

"I didn't need you to save me," I say finally. "I just needed you to be honest."

"I know."

He steps closer, slow enough that I can move if I want to—but I don't.

"I spent half my life following orders," he says. "It's how you survive in this world. You don't question. You don't feel. You just endure." His voice drops, barely more than a whisper. "But you make that impossible."

I meet his gaze. "Good."

A small, broken laugh slips out of him—like he hasn't remembered how to for years.

Then, quieter: "I care about you, Elia. More than I should. And that's the problem."

The words don't sound like a confession. They sound like a warning.

He looks away again, jaw flexing. "If Lucien ever suspects how deep that runs, he'll use it. Against both of us. So if I seem cold, if I follow an order that looks like betrayal—it's not because you don't matter. It's because you do."

The forest wind sighs through the broken dome, scattering dust across the floor.

For a long moment, neither of us speaks. Then I stand, closing the distance between us until only inches remain. His breath hitches.

"I don't need protection," I say, steady now. "Just the truth."

He nods once, slow and solemn. "Then that's what you'll get."

The air hums between us—fragile, alive.

He doesn't reach for me. He just stands there, storm-gray eyes reflecting the firelight from far below, like a man finally stepping out of his own shadow.

And for the first time, I see the truth beneath the soldier:
Cassian didn't leave me to obey.
He left me to keep me breathing.

It doesn't make the hurt vanish. But it makes it real.

When I turn to leave, he doesn't stop me. Only says, softly,
"If following orders saved your life once, I'll break them next time to make sure you live."

I don't look back.
But for the first time since the tower, the weight in my chest eases—
not gone, just lighter.

And as the night folds around the ridge, I realize the Hollow has changed again.
Not safer.
Not quieter.
Just more human.

Chapter 23

All Eyes on Crimson

The Dominion doesn't whisper when it wants blood. It bellows.

By dawn, the Hollow hums like a hornet nest kicked open. Rebels spill from their huts, clustering around the patchwork screens Lennox wired into old Dominion receivers. Static crackles, then clears.

The insignia blazes—white on black. The Chancellor's voice follows, crisp and merciless: "Citizens of New Virelia, and all cities beyond. Be vigilant."

Her face flickers into focus, polished like glass, untouched by age, carved from stone and steel. Dominion banners loom behind her.

And then another image—my image.
Me, caught mid-breath, wrist lifted, Crimson bright.

"Wanted," she intones. "Elia Dareth. Crimson anomaly. Dead or alive."

The word WANTED glares red across the screen.

But she doesn't stop there.
"Elia Dareth is guilty of treasonous acts against the Dominion. She orchestrated the bombing of Breaker Tower, resulting in thirty-four civilian deaths."

The Hollow gasps. My chest locks.

"Lies," Tova hisses beside me.

The Chancellor's voice remains unflinching. "She infiltrated the Marking Archives, corrupting data records. She seeks to destabilize order through deceit. She must be brought to justice—for the safety of all."

Images cycle: rubble, blurred bodies, smoke thick as storm clouds. Labeled: **BREAKER TOWER MASSACRE.** Then my face again, my Mark blazing like evidence.

Their story is clean. Polished. Poisoned.
And I am the villain.

Couriers stumble into the clearing, breathless, half-panicked.
"West city—round-ups. Every Crimson detained."
"South markets—executions. Public. No trials."

The Hollow shakes with unease. Some glare at me; others look away as if I've already doomed them.

Lennox slams his mug down, coffee sloshing. "This is their game. Twist truth, tie the rope, hang us with it."
Tova spits into the dirt. "And the people will believe it. Fear's always easier than freedom."

Fire churns hot in my chest—anger, grief, fury braided together. I step forward, into the clearing, into the ring of flickering screens.

"Then we give them something else to believe," I say, voice steady, rising.

Heads turn. Lucien's eyes narrow, warning in every line of his stance, but I don't stop.

"They call me murderer, traitor, curse. They'll keep doing it until the world forgets the truth—unless we show them. Not whispers. Not rumors. Truth. On every tower, every node, every screen."

I raise my wrist, Crimson and flare burning bright. "They wanted my face to be a warning. Fine. Let's make it a reckoning."

The Hollow holds its breath.

Tova mutters, "God help us, she means it."
Lennox's grin cuts sharp. "Hijack their Spine."

The word lands like thunder.

The Spine: Dominion's master satellite, its signal feeding every city, every citizen. Untouchable. Unthinkable.
To reach it would be suicide.
To win it would be revolution.

Lucien's jaw tightens. "You're insane."
"Maybe," I say. "But if all eyes are on me, then I'll make them see."

The plan sparks faster than fear can root. Lennox dives into his code, muttering, twitching with caffeine

153

and adrenaline.

"I can weave the virus through their relay lines. Once it hits the Spine, it'll cascade. Every channel, every screen—ours. Two minutes, maybe less, before they shut us down."

Tova drags her whetstone across her blade, sparks flashing. "Two minutes is enough to bleed truth. If we burn after, so be it."

And then Cassian moves.
Not fast. Not loud. Just certain—through the crowd, through the chaos—until he's in front of me.

His presence stills everything around us.

He doesn't argue, doesn't call me reckless. He just presses something small and cold into my palm. A battered *holotransmitter.*

"Use it if we're cut off," he says, low enough for only me to hear. "It's synced to my signal only."

I glance down. The casing's dented, the Dominion emblem scratched out but still faint beneath the metal. "Cassian, this is your command link. You're supposed to keep this."

"I know."

The words come out softer than I expect. His hand lingers over mine, fingers brushing the edge of the device—just enough to steady it. Or maybe me.

"If anything goes wrong," he continues quietly, "you reach me. Not Lucien. Not the Hollow. Me."

I look up, caught by the weight behind his voice. "Why?"

His gaze doesn't waver. "Because I don't trust him to keep you alive."

The words land heavier than the transmitter itself.

I search his face, trying to find the commander's mask, but it's gone. What's left looks almost... raw. Tired. Human.

"You're supposed to follow his orders," I whisper.

"I did," Cassian says, voice taut. "And look where it got us."

He steps closer, low enough that his next words scrape just above a breath. "If he tries to use you again, I'll stop him. No matter the order."

My throat tightens. I want to ask *why,* but I already know the answer lives in the things he doesn't say.

Lucien's shadow crosses the firelight, his tone razor-edged. "You two done?"

Cassian straightens immediately, the moment folding back into command. "Ready when you are."

But as Lucien turns away, Cassian's hand brushes mine again—quick, unnoticeable, deliberate. "Keep it close," he murmurs. "Even if I'm not."

I nod, unable to find words.

He nods once back, jaw set. Then he's gone, swallowed by the blur of motion and orders.

Lucien calls out new assignments. Lennox barks coordinates. The Hollow comes alive again—voices, weapons, defiance.

But the world feels quieter where Cassian's hand just was.

Night falls heavy. The transmitter sits in my palm, warm from his touch. Its faint blue pulse beats steady, syncing to the rhythm of my Mark.

The Dominion wants my face across every screen? Then they'll have it.

Not their villain.
Me.
And if Cassian's right—if this is suicide—then at least I'll burn on my own terms.

Chapter 24

The Rebellion Rises

The Spine looms like a metal god.
It claws up from the old Capitol ruins — ribs of black
steel, antennae stabbing the clouds, wires humming
with other people's orders. The sky above it glows
faintly red, as if even the stars have learned to bleed
for the Dominion.

Tonight, we try to steal its voice.

The Hollow moves like a single heartbeat. Rebels
gather in the valley shadows — a tide of faces and
firelight. Fighters from the Hollow. Tova's medics,
armor patched with old scars. Lennox dragging his
rigs like spare limbs, goggles reflecting the glow of his
makeshift terminals. The Remnants from the Grove
— farmers, traders, children with flare-marks on their
wrists and the hard set of those who have nothing left
to lose.

Not just soldiers. People.

They look to me.
The fugitive. The liar. The spark.

I lift my wrist, and the flare burns crimson in the
dark.
"Tonight," I tell them, "we don't just break things."
The firelight catches their eyes, one by one. "We
show them the truth."

The roar that follows shakes the night.

Cassian's gaze finds mine across the crowd. Storm-gray, steady — but the tightness in his jaw betrays what he doesn't say. He knows what this night will cost. Maybe that's why he doesn't stop me. Maybe that's why he stays so close.

The March

We move out before midnight.
The valley swells with motion — boots sinking into ash, whispers muffled under fog. The cold cuts like glass, and every breath hangs visible, proof we're still alive, for now.

Cassian takes point, silent as a shadow. He signals with two fingers, and his strike team melts into the dark. I follow with Lennox, Tova, and a group of Hollow fighters, hearts pounding in unison.

The closer we get, the more the air hums — that strange Dominion frequency, half electric, half alive. The Spine feeds on it, pulses with it. It's like walking toward a storm that can hear you coming.

"Perimeter drones ahead," Cassian murmurs through the comm.
He drops to a knee, rifle glinting faintly. One by one, the drones drop too — blue eyes dimming to black, metal shells crumpling into the grass.

"Clear," he says, voice tight.

Tova's squad rushes forward, packs heavy with charges. They work fast — attaching shaped explosives to gates that used to guard the Capitol's heart. "Five seconds," she warns.

The explosions roll through the night like thunder. The gates bloom open, metal petals curling outward. Smoke spills across the field. Rebels surge through the gaps.

And then the Spine awakens.

Black-armored enforcers spill from the structure — visors cutting through the dark with white light. Gunfire tears through the valley, slicing air. Sparks rain down like violent stars.

Civilians scatter for cover. Cassian doesn't. He moves through the chaos like a storm given shape — each step deliberate, each shot controlled. He shields the medics without a word, pivots just enough that a beam meant for me finds the wall instead.

I run beside him, dagger in one hand, the transmitter clutched tight in the other. The world is noise — shouting, smoke, the whine of machines — and still, Cassian's voice cuts through it all:

"Stay with me."

Not a command. A promise.

Inside the Spine

Inside, the air tastes metallic, sharp with ozone. Corridors stretch long and sterile, marked with the Dominion emblem. Every surface hums faintly, alive with current.

Lennox drops to his knees beside a control panel, fingers already flying. "Jammers everywhere," he mutters. "They'll shut the feed before it even leaves the grid. Give me three minutes."

Tova's voice is flat. "You've got two."

Cassian glances at me. "Stay behind me."

I don't.
I step forward instead, tracing the metal wall where data pulses like veins of light. The Spine isn't just steel; it's alive with memory — every broadcast, every command, every lie the Dominion ever told, archived here like holy scripture.

The first jammer goes in a cloud of sparks. The second fries under Lennox's code. The third fights back — a surge of white noise that knocks the lights into chaos.

"Contact!" Tova yells.
Reinforcements pour through the hall — a flood of black helmets and gunfire.

Cassian's shoulder collides with mine as he pulls me back behind a fallen console. "Stay down!"
He fires over my head, each shot precise, each breath measured. But I see it — the fear in his movements,

the way he keeps himself between me and the oncoming storm.

Tova takes a hit to her side. She snarls through the pain, dragging Ren's hand to the wound. "Tourniquet. Now."
"I said keep pressure!"
"Do it anyway!"

The battle eats seconds like fire eats air.

The Core

Finally, the corridor spills open into a massive chamber — a cathedral of light and machinery. At its center, a sphere of glass and alloy floats, veins of blue and gold running across its surface like a living heart.

Lennox stumbles forward, awe breaking through exhaustion. "The central core," he whispers. "I can thread the virus from here. Once it hits, the Spine's theirs — all of it."

He glances at me. "You'll have two minutes of control. After that, Dominion override kicks in."

"Then make it live," I say.

Cassian steps forward, disbelief in his tone. "Elia—"

"If they want *every eye on me*," I interrupt, climbing the dais, "then let them see me."

The sphere's surface mirrors me back — dirt-smeared, blood-slick, human. I press the transmitter against the node.

For a heartbeat, nothing. Then the world blinks black.

Every Dominion channel — every propaganda feed, every billboard and surveillance drone — goes silent.

And then my face fills the screens.

The Broadcast

No filters. No helmets. No edits. Just me.

"My name is Elia Dareth," I say into every living room, every market screen, every watchtower across the Dominion. "They built a story to scare you. Murderer. Traitor. A Crimson curse. They lied."

Even here, the room stills. The battle outside fades beneath the hum of the broadcast.

"Marks were meant to warn," I say, voice trembling but clear, "not to chain. The Dominion turned them into leashes. They tell you who to fear, who to hate, who to erase. But the algorithm isn't prophecy. It's control."

The data sphere flickers. Static curls at the edges of my reflection. Time slips.

"I am proof it can be wrong," I continue. "I survived every prediction they made about me. And that means you can too."

Outside, explosions boom — the rebellion fighting to buy me seconds. I can hear Tova shouting, Lennox cursing, Cassian barking orders. Still, I speak.

"You are more than data. More than the number they assign you. More than the fate they sell you. You are choice. And choice is what they fear most."

The doors blast inward. Smoke rolls through the chamber.

Cassian bursts through it, eyes wild, blood streaked across his cheek. "Elia, we have to go!"

I don't move.

He crosses the floor under fire, grabs my arm, and pulls me down just as a round shatters the console. The force sends the transmitter skidding. I snatch it before it falls into the crackling debris.

"Cassian—"

"Now!" he shouts. "The feed's collapsing—"

But I shake free, planting my feet again on the dais. "Not yet."

The feed flickers — Dominion override creeping in like black frost.

I lift my wrist to the sphere, letting the flare burn through the static. "They can shut down screens," I say into the chaos, "but they can't shut down sight. Look. See. Choose."

The sound fractures. The image distorts.

For a few last seconds, the Dominion's networks show a living, breathing person instead of a regime.

Aftermath

The feed dies with a sharp crack — power surging back through the Spine's veins. The shockwave knocks me to the floor. Sparks rain from the ceiling.

Cassian's arms are around me before I can move. His breath hits my ear — harsh, desperate.
"I told you to run."

"You knew I wouldn't."

He doesn't argue. His grip just tightens, dragging me up. "Then I'll make sure you can't die standing still."

We stumble through the collapsing corridor. Lennox is limping, Tova half-carried between two rebels. Smoke chokes the hallways. Outside, the valley is fire and thunder.

But something has changed in the air. The Dominion channels may have gone dark — but the silence feels different now. Like waiting. Like holding breath.

Somewhere beyond the smoke, I imagine the people watching — kitchens, markets, bunkers — seeing that final flicker of truth. Seeing me.

This isn't victory. Not yet.
Flames will take houses. Blood will stain roads.

But something irreversible has begun.
Something the Dominion can't predict.
Something the Hollow could never contain.

Cassian's hand finds mine as we break into the open air. He doesn't speak. Doesn't have to. The firelight paints the side of his face — equal parts soldier and survivor.

And for one suspended moment, I let myself believe the same thing I told the world:
That we are more than the story they wrote for us.

The night roars. The Spine burns.
And I do not look away.

Chapter 25

Crimson Rising

Two minutes.
That's all it took.

Lennox gave me two minutes inside the Spine's core
— two minutes of stolen air. Two minutes, and a
nation trembles.

Screens go black.
The Dominion's endless loop of armor and parades,
of smiling children in Marking Halls, of Crimsons
quietly erased — all silenced.
Then my face fills the void: scarred, ash-streaked,
wrist lifted, flare burning bright.

What I said — *I wasn't marked to die. I was marked to
decide.*
It echoes into every market, every courtyard, every
Marking Hall where children sit with bare wrists and
waiting eyes.

The Chancellor's voice cuts out mid-sentence. His
polished certainty flickers. In its place: a question. A
possibility. A choice.

And across New Virelia, people begin to do things
they were taught never to do.

In the east, sleeves roll up, flare marks painted in soot
and blood. Crimsons walk into the streets, shouting
the words back.

In the west, parents tear their children from lines, smashing scanners, ripping banners down.
In the southern mines, workers drop their tools and lift painted arms as enforcers arrive.
And in the Capitol's shadow, people pour into the squares — not with weapons first, but with voices.

Choice! Choice! Choice!

The chant ripples like wildfire through a city built on silence.
Soldiers hesitate. Visors tilt. And something small, fragile, impossible begins to spread — doubt.

The Dominion, which built an empire on prediction, stumbles.
And the machine that was never meant to tremble begins to.

The Fall

Inside the Spine, chaos becomes concrete. The air is smoke and sparks and screaming alarms. Lennox's virus burns like fever through the system, wires spitting light.
Cassian's shout cuts through the roar — sharp, commanding, terrified. "Fall back!"
Tova drags a half-conscious fighter to cover. Lennox slams his hand against the console, trying to stabilize the feed, but it's already unraveling.

Then — pain.
A rifle butt connects with my skull. The world folds, sound drains.

When I wake, the light is wrong.

Chains bite my wrists. My knees drag against broken
concrete. The air tastes of ash and iron.
They don't waste time.

The Dominion drags me through the ruined Capitol
— past toppled statues, past streets flooded with
smoke and ash, past screens that still flash my image:
WANTED.
Not propaganda anymore. Not history either. *Live.*

They shove me onto a stage welded over cracked
stone. The crowd is forced to watch.
A soldier presses a rifle to the back of my skull. The
Chancellor's voice spills from loudspeakers —
smooth, rehearsed, venom in velvet.

"Here stands Elia Dareth. The anomaly. The traitor.
Her death will restore order."

Faces blur in the smoke. Some are terrified. Some
defiant. Most just tired.

Then — through the chaos — I see him.

Cassian.
Storm-gray eyes cutting through the press. He's
fighting forward, shoving through black armor,
shouting until his voice breaks. His rifle's gone. His
hands bleed. He moves like a man who has already
lost too much and refuses to lose this too.

The rifle digs deeper into my neck. My pulse hammers in my throat.

"They said my death would keep you safe," I call out, voice raw but steady.

The crowd stirs — a ripple of confusion, curiosity, memory.

I lift my chin. Chains rattle.
"But I was never meant to die."
My words find rhythm, the rhythm finds power.
"I was meant to decide. And so are you."

A breathless silence spreads, taut and trembling.

"Kill me," I say louder, eyes fixed on the soldier behind me. "Kill me and they'll rise. Let me live, and they already have."

Something fractures.
The soldier's hands shake. The barrel wavers. His breath stutters — one moment, one heartbeat — and he lowers the gun.

A gasp runs through the crowd. Then a voice. Then another.
"Choice!"
"Choice!"
"Choice!"

It spreads like fire through dry grass.

Around the square, rifles drop. Soldiers glance at each other, then to the people they were meant to silence. One removes his visor. Then another. Defectors. A tide turning.

The Chancellor's voice snaps back, panicked. "Obey your orders! Restore control!"
But static eats the edges of his words. His voice falters beneath the rising chant.

And then the square explodes into motion.

From the far edge — smoke and flash — Lucien appears with Hollow reinforcements. Not all rebels, not just rebels. Remnants. Workers. Ordinary people who decided walls could fall.
They surge forward. The Dominion line cracks.

For the first time in memory, the square belongs to no one's algorithm.

Cassian reaches the stage. His hands are cut, his jaw bruised, his uniform half torn. He slices through my chains with a blade scavenged from a fallen guard. Metal falls away.

He catches my wrists — gently this time, not as a soldier but as someone afraid to hurt what he's holding. His eyes meet mine, storm-gray and exhausted and alive.

"I told you," he says, voice rough, low enough for only me. "I care anyway."

The words hit harder than any blow.
I want to answer, to tell him that care is what doomed us and what saved us both — but all that comes out is a breath that feels like forgiveness.

For a heartbeat, everything stops — the roar, the gunfire, the panic. Just us on the cracked stone, the Dominion burning below.

The Uprising

The Capitol fractures.
Banners rip from their poles. Screens go dark and stay that way because there's no power left to keep the lies lit.

People shout, cry, sing. Some climb statues to tear them down.
Someone sets a Dominion flag on fire. Someone else kneels and presses a soot-hand to a child's face, smearing it into a flare-mark like a blessing.

It isn't victory. Not yet.
It's something wilder. Realer.

Tova limps toward us, blood on her sleeve and laughter on her lips. "Still breathing," she mutters, collapsing onto a step. "Against all odds."
Lennox is beside her, trembling but grinning, his tablet cracked and sparking. "They'll never scrub that feed. It's in the archive now. The virus made sure of it."

I stare up at the broken Spine in the distance — its tower split open, sparks still dripping into the dark. "What we started there," I whisper, "they can't unsee it."

Cassian steps beside me. His hand brushes mine — a small, deliberate thing. Not to claim. To steady. To say *I'm still here.*

"You gave them a choice," he says quietly. "Now they'll have to decide what to do with it."

"*We* gave them one," I correct.

He almost smiles — the smallest tilt of a mouth that's forgotten how. "You always have to share the blame, don't you?"

"Always."

His hand lingers for a heartbeat longer, then drops. But the warmth stays.

The Reckoning

This is not tidy.
It is smoke and blood and splintered wood and small mercies. Houses burn. Roads choke with rubble. People die. That's the truth of rebellion. The cost is never neat.

But the thing that began in the Spine — the sight of one person saying *no* — it spreads. It cannot be unsaid.

The Chancellor's networks fail city by city. Crimsons rise. Ambers march. Greens hide them in basements. The Dominion tries to count us again — and fails.

The numbers don't fit anymore.

I stand on that welded stone with the flare still warm against my skin and Cassian beside me, the square a blur of movement and smoke and song.

They called me anomaly. Glitch. Curse. Spark.
Words meant to cage me.
Now they mean something else.

Reckoning.

We didn't end the Dominion in two minutes. Not even close.
But we cracked the first wall. We burned a line in the sky. We gave people a glimpse of choice — and once you've seen another life, you start to walk toward it.

Cassian's hand finds my shoulder, grounding me. He doesn't kneel. He doesn't have to.
I don't need a savior.
And he no longer needs to be one.

We stand together — two people remade by the same fire.

Above us, the Capitol smolders. Smoke curls up into the bruised sky. The ashes scatter in the wind, red as embers.

And for the first time, it feels like hope.

Chapter 26

If I Die, Let It Matter

The Dominion didn't collapse in a single shout.
It fractured — thin, hairline cracks spreading until the
whole structure began to splinter.

The blackout at the Spine was the first break.
After the feed went dark, orders unraveled. Enforcers
drifted from their posts — some vanishing into alleys,
some joining the very crowds they once controlled.
The Chancellor's voice flickered across the screens —
one final command, cut short — and then silence, like
a candle snuffed mid-breath.

Cities changed the way weather does: sudden,
unpredictable, impossible to stop.
Crimson, Amber, Blue, Green — people rolled up
sleeves and painted flare sigils over old marks in soot
and chalk.
Parents pulled their children from queues. Teenagers
looked at scanners and shrugged.
Choice spread faster than control could contain it.

Councils formed almost overnight. Farmers elected
elders to divide rations. Engineers in the west fixed
water pumps without waiting for clearance. The
southern settlements declared themselves free. And
across the land, people started speaking in ways they'd
forgotten they knew how to.

The Capitol Square — once a stage for Markings and
executions — became a market of voices. Fires

burned in barrels. Traders haggled over seeds and wire. Someone shouted about rebuilding schools.
It wasn't peace. Not yet.
But it wasn't chains either.

Inside the ruined halls, commanders argued deep into the night. Lucien presided with his calm precision; Tova leaned against a column with her arm bandaged and her sarcasm sharp as ever; Lennox survived on coffee and defiance, code bleeding from his fingertips. The Remnants sat among them — quiet but unshakable — reminding us that memory mattered more than monuments.

They argued about structure, defense, medicine, fairness.
Whether to build walls or wells first.
It was messy. Exhausting. Real.

I listened more than I spoke. My two minutes on the Spine had cracked something open, and now it wasn't mine to control.
Choice, I was learning, also meant stepping back.
Letting others decide.
Harder than any battle. Scarier too.

When night settled, I walked the square.
I saw people barter bread, stitch wounds, teach children to tie their first flare scarves.
I watched an ex-enforcer hand his rifle to a girl with grease-stained fingers and say softly, "You walk with us now, not over us."
Small moments — but each one dangerous in the best way.

We hadn't fixed the world. Not even close.
Buildings still smoked. Food was scarce. Too many
names would never be spoken again.
But the air had changed. It tasted sharp. Possible.

Sometimes, when the fires hissed and the stars broke
through the haze, I thought about dying — about that
crack of pain, that instant when the world had tried to
rewrite me into silence.
If I die tomorrow, I only want it to mean something
— not a headline or a legend. Just a beginning. A
habit. People choosing for themselves.

Lucien mapped supply routes while I sketched
schoolhouses on scraps of paper. Lennox muttered
code until the satellite link stuttered awake.
Tova taught first aid to anyone willing to learn.
The Remnants told history from memory alone.
Choice multiplied into something loud and stubborn
and human.

Elia's Journal

*I sit on the cracked stone of the Capitol steps, writing
with ink that smudges and paper that's half burned. I write
because everyone else seems to have a plan or a purpose, and I
need a place where the edges don't cut.*
I'm not a weapon. Not a warning.
I am loud.
I keep saying it until it stops sounding like a lie.
Maybe someone will find these pages. Maybe they'll be

used to start a fire. Maybe a child will smear soot over the words and laugh. It doesn't matter. They're mine.

On the fifth night, I find Cassian sitting on the steps. His posture is different now — less armor, more exhaustion. Below us, the square begins to stir: kids chase each other, rebels trade with farmers, laughter sparks through the smoke. For a while, there are no orders. Only people.

I sit beside him, close enough to feel his warmth but far enough to keep the quiet between us.
"I might still die," I whisper. He looks at me, but I don't let him answer. "But it won't be the story they wrote."
The flare on my wrist burns soft and gold, like a small hearth instead of a curse. "It'll be mine."

The dawn comes slow. Pale light spills across the broken Capitol, gilding what's left of the marble and soot. Cassian's still beside me, the night's chill woven through his jacket. When he speaks, it's barely above a breath.

"You changed everything," he says.
"I survived," I answer. "That's all."
He shakes his head. "No. You taught them how."

He turns his wrist — no flare, just skin and scars.
"Maybe one day we'll all get to decide who we are without someone else branding it first."

"Maybe one day we already have."

He looks at me then — really looks. The kind of look
that carries both promise and warning, and I realize
how fragile peace can feel when it's right beside you.

At sunrise, children lift their wrists to the sky —
marks glowing in every color.
Not verdicts anymore.
Not property.
Just choice.

The sun climbs higher, catching the jagged edge of
the Capitol dome until it looks almost whole again.
For the first time, the light feels like it belongs to us.

Two days later, a messenger reaches me from the
northern convoy.
Survivors had been found near the river — scattered
families from the first raids.
Among them was my aunt.

I rode out at dawn to meet her.
When I saw her — face thinner but eyes still fierce —
it was like a thread I didn't know was missing snapped
back into place. She'd hidden in the mountain
tunnels, helping the wounded, keeping stories alive in
the dark.

When she saw the flare on my wrist, she smiled.
"Your mother would've liked that color," she said.

We stood there for a long time, saying nothing.
Just breathing the same free air.
She's safe now. And that word — *safe* — feels like the
rarest kind of miracle.

Elia's Journal

The smoke is clearing. The world feels raw and unsteady, like a song that hasn't found its rhythm yet. But there's music under it — quiet, waiting to grow.

Cassian says we'll rebuild the Spine one day — not as a cage, but as a bridge.
Lucien talks about councils. Tova about medicine. Lennox about stars. My aunt tells stories around the fire — the kind that make people remember who they are.

I don't know where I'll go next. Maybe I'll stay long enough to see something bloom. Maybe I'll follow the river north until the sky feels wide again.

Whatever happens, these pages will outlive me.

If someone finds them — know this:
I was marked once.
Now, I'm simply alive.
If I die tomorrow, let it matter.
Let it mean we chose our own ending.
Let it mean we began again.

Cassian finds me later, still writing. He leans against the pillar beside me, arms folded, expression caught somewhere between wary and gentle.
"Still keeping score?"
"Just remembering," I say. "Someone has to."
He studies me, then the pages. "Then remember this too," he murmurs.

When I glance up, he's already looking past the horizon, but his hand brushes mine — deliberate, grounding.

"None of this happens without you," he says. "Not the fire. Not the choice. Not me still standing."

The words settle between us like embers that refuse to die.

I close the notebook and tuck it into my jacket. "Then we stand together," I tell him.

He nods once. "Until the next storm."

And as the wind shifts, carrying the scent of ash and rain, I believe him.
The world is still cracked, still bleeding — but there's light in the fractures.

Somewhere beyond the smoke, the first green shoots break through the blackened earth.

Crimson still rising.

Epilogue

Ash in the Wind

The Capitol is quieter now—
smoke settling over the ruins, not flames.

Banners are gone, their emblems torn down or
scorched to nothing. But their echo still hums
beneath the stone, faint and electric, like a ghost
signal refusing to die.

Elia stands where the stage once was—the place they
meant to execute her. The metal is still scarred from
rifle fire, streaked with soot and memory.
The crowds are gone. The shouts, the chants, the
rebellion's roar—all faded into the long breath after
war.

Cassian finds her there, as always, when the world
turns quiet.

He doesn't speak at first. Just watches the wind tug
her hair across her face, watches her fingers brush the
flare mark on her wrist as if she's testing whether it's
still real.

"You should rest," he says finally. His voice is rough
from smoke and sleepless nights.

She shakes her head. "Rest feels wrong. Like stopping
means forgetting."

Cassian's jaw tightens. "We can't fight forever."

Elia's eyes lift to the skyline—to the broken towers glinting under the rising sun. "We might have to." A faint smile flickers. "Just... not the same fight."

He steps closer, close enough that their shadows overlap against the metal floor. "You changed everything, Elia."

She looks at him then, tired but steady. "No. *We* did." Her gaze drifts back toward the horizon, where columns of smoke twist into the morning clouds. "The Dominion's gone, Cassian. But something's still out there. I can feel it."

He follows her stare. "Leftovers?"

"Remnants. Codes. Secrets." Her voice softens, distant. "This wasn't just control. It was built too carefully for that. Someone wanted it to last."

He doesn't argue. He's learned not to—not when her instincts turn sharp.
Instead, he slips something into her hand. A small metal disk, scratched and cold.

"I found this," he says. "Lennox pulled it from a collapsed relay near the Capitol's edge. Thought you'd want to see it."

She turns it over.
A Dominion crest—half melted, edges warped—and beneath the soot, faint letters:

PROJECT DARETH

Her breath catches. The world tilts, just slightly.
"That's my name."

Cassian's eyes narrow. "Could be a coincidence."

She looks up at him, her expression unreadable.
"It never is."

Wind cuts through the square, scattering flakes of ash
like snow.
Elia curls her fingers around the disk and tucks it into
her jacket pocket, the metal warm against her heart.

When she finally speaks, it's barely a whisper.

"This isn't over."

Cassian studies her—the fire behind her exhaustion,
the way her voice steadies even when her hands
shake.
He nods once, almost to himself.

"Then neither am I."

They stand there as dawn climbs over the ruins—two
silhouettes against a new and fragile world, the ashes
of the old drifting around them like the first snowfall
of a future that hasn't yet chosen what to become.

Far beneath the Capitol, deep under collapsed tunnels
and drowned circuits, a flicker of light blinks to life
on an old Dominion console.

SYSTEM RESTORE INITIATED.
FILE LOCATED: PROJECT DARETH /
CHRYSALIS PROTOCOL.

The hum grows louder. The screen stabilizes.

And the Dominion—or something wearing its skin—
begins to wake.

END OF BOOK ONE

THE MARKED: CRIMSON RISING

BOOK TWO COMING SOON

THE MARKED: ASHFALL

Every revolution has its price. Some are paid in truth.

www.ingramcontent.com/pod-product-compliance
Lightning Source LLC
Chambersburg PA
CBHW060930120626
46557CB00003B/935